Copyright © 2018

L. J. Thorburn

(pen name Blair Coleman)

First Published Oct 2018
ISBN: 9781091399419

To Gemma
Lots of Love
& Hugs
Blair Coleman

Through My Tainted Eye

by Blair Coleman

Dedications

It goes without saying, that the biggest dedication will always be reserved for my family. Without their ongoing support and understanding, I would not be where I am today.

I don't just write books – though, I would love to – I hold down a full-time job, have a little side thing that I do for other authors and generally try to have some form a social life with friends and loved one. None of this would be possible without my family.

This past year, as I've been writing this book, has been a testament to my willpower, my control and my sanity. It has thrown me one thing after another, and there have been times I've wanted to give up and move away where no-one knows me. I'm sure we're all had those days! My family is the reason I keep going, they're the reason I get up in the morning, they're the reason I go to work – so that I can earn money to shower them with materialistic appreciation when the occasion calls. They are my reason for more things than I know how to list.

I also want to thank my partner. He's probably one of the highest causes of my stress!! Both directly, and indirectly. But he keeps me going, too. He might not know it, and maybe he will realise it if he ever reads this, but, despite what gets hurled our way, I love him with all my heart.

My little Beta group are also deserving of my thanks. Without them, I would have missed a hell of a lot of typos, grammar cock ups, and many other things that I don't like seeing when I read! They encourage me, and offer me all the support that they can.

My friends over at 'The Hive,' you know who you are. It's a brand new adventure we've all started in that group, and I really do think it's been paying off. I see good things going forward, and without you girls, it wouldn't have happened.

To all the event organizers who allow me to sit at a table, in a venue of their choice, and sign my babies. Without you guys, networking and marketing would be a harder ballache than it already is. I appreciate every opportunity.

If I've missed anyone out, then you have my sincerest apologies. Just know that I appreciate and value every inch if support and all the kind words you've ever offered me during my writing career.

I love you all!

Preface

As with a couple of my erotic novels (mostly unpublished at this moment in time), this one started as a 10,000-word short story for a publisher's anthology submission. For one reason or another, that anthology never materialised. Through My Tainted eyes then spent some years sat in a folder, going from laptop to laptop as I changed from one to another over that time.

I decided that I needed something else to add to my erotic collection, having only two to date. I figured, I'd aim for another novella, somewhere in the region of 25,000 words. Of course, the bulk of the story was mapped out, but the more I read, the more I was thankful that it never made it into the anthology. It needed to much more substance, something meatier, filthier, more gripping.

So, we are now sat at circa 50,000 words, with the hopes of being able to, possibly, continue with the MC one day.

This is a standalone – it was always intended to be a standalone. But I have a tendency to develop my characters, so much so, that I want to do more with them. This may likely be no exception.

I hope that you enjoy reading this, as much as I enjoyed writing it.

Here goes …

Prologue

Tessa could still hear their stomach-churning screams, could still feel their untainted, palpable pained fear... could still smell the stale stink of sweat, blood and something far more contemptible in the air.

From inside her cargo-prison, she knew it would not be long before they came for her, too. It would not be long before it would be her screams ringing in her ears - or in those of some other unfortunate.

She couldn't remember how long she'd been inside her steel confines. One day, two... three, perhaps? She still wore the same dress from the night they stole her away from the life she knew. Though, now, it bore the stains and stenches of her terror at the mercy of the men who kidnapped her.

There were other girls, at first. But, one by one, they were taken by muscled men in leather masks. They stank of cigars and rum. It would be a smell she would never forget, a smell she would flinch at if a slight touch of the aroma permeated her nostrils ... if she were to survive this.

Being the last in the crate, her time would be soon.

She spent her hours wondering why the girls were never returned to their prison. Where were they now? Were they free of their torment? She doubted it; who, in their right mind, would commit such atrocities, only to then release those who were victim to it. They would go to the police, surely. These men would know that much.

So, then what? Were they all dead?

The notion made her wretch, caused fresh tears to add to those already staining her cold, clammy cheeks.

When thoughts of the others weren't plaguing her mind, she would think of her family. They would be worried, frightened out of their wits, concocting stories of what had happened to her. Some of which would likely be true. They would be looking for her; doing everything in their power to have their youngest daughter returned to them, safe and sound.

Were her kidnappers demanding a ransom? Would she live long enough, even if her family paid it?

In the first day or two, Tessa couldn't stop shaking. The fear wracked and tortured her body; unrelenting, it weakened her limbs, her mind, her soul. The endless scenarios made her sick to her stomach. She cried almost every minute of every hour.

But now, there were no more tears. She couldn't even be sure if still felt the same fear. Her body sagged against the cold metal, spent, drained, ready and willing to succumb to whatever fate would befall her.

Or, so she thought.

On day five, as far as she could gather, the inevitable happened - they came for her. Three of them, dressed in black, their masks in place.

As they approached her, her stomach turned. She let out a strangled cry, tried to shuffle as far back as she could, away from them. But she could go no further, and, between them, they hauled her to her feet as she tried to make her body heavy, by dropping the weight of her legs beneath her.

It didn't work. Two took a meaty grip of her biceps, while the other hefted her feet off the ground, securing them under his powerful arms.

She writhed in their grasp, determined, now, not to deliver herself so easily to them. She didn't want to die, didn't want to know what waited for her on the other side of the container doors.

She noticed the dark hues of purples, blues and pinks of the sky first; the signs of an approaching twilight. Stars littered the heavens, like millions of twinkling diamonds; an alluring sight, lighting a pathway as if they knew she would be following it soon enough.

The men dragged her through a heavy, dirty curtain, and then through another, roughly throwing her onto a makeshift bed.

"Get dressed," one of them barked at her, his foreign accent light. He opened a bin liner and threw fresh garments at her. "Make yourself pretty." He nodded his head in the direction of a crumbling vanity station, which housed a small assortment of cheap face wipes and makeup.

"For what?" Tessa eyed the items, not much wanting to hear the answer.

Just as well; none of the men gave her one, as they walked out and left her alone. "Ten minutes," one called back.

And again, for what?

She didn't wear makeup, nor would she be putting it on for these men, or any other. She did, however, use more than enough of the wipes to clean the filth from her face, neck and other areas of her body. Yet, still she felt dirty.

When the cloths started to come off relatively clean, she turned her attention to the bag of clothes and fresh underwear. Without pausing for thought as to their need, she rushed over, changing quickly. Most of the items were made of much less material than her current attire, and only when she noticed, did she start to wonder why.

Standing only in her own bra, and clean, lace panties, she jumped, when the curtains to her homemade bedroom shifted.

In walked a middle-aged, bearded man of, perhaps, Turkish or Greek descent. The leer he gave her, as he looked her up and down, made her shiver.

Tessa crossed her arms over her chest, but that only served to offer the man new pleasures, as he gawked at her cleavage with wide, hungry eyes.

“Stay away from me,” she tried to tell him, her dry voice a croaking whisper. Panic surged through her; a fearful thought of what this man might do to her scared her more than death. She didn’t want to be defiled like this, didn’t want to feel the pain – both physical and emotional – that would be wrought on her.

The man said nothing, as he advanced closer, the lewd smile never leaving his face. When he got close enough, he reached out a hairy, grubby hand, grabbing Tessa's arm before pulling her closer.

She let out a squeal, tears escaping the corners of her eyes. She felt powerless with no escape; no-where to run as she glared into his unkind eyes.

Using both of his hands, the man pushed Tessa, backwards, onto the mattress, before removing his shirt and jeans.

Now, she knew for sure.

Her survival instinct kicked in, and she screamed, scrambling on the bed to right herself. No way – no way would she give this foul, degrading beast her virtue. She would rather die.

Launching himself at her, the man pinned her down, his power far outweighing her own as she struggled beneath him, scrunching her eyes closed, turning her head to avoid his lips as he tried to litter her face with animalistic kisses. He smelled of cooking grease and cigarettes.

Using his determined strength, he seized both of her tiny wrists in one meaty grip above her head. With the other hand, he fumbled with his underwear, shimmying it down his thighs, exposing himself above her. Roughly, he parted her legs, despite her strong-willed protests. When she clamped them shut, he pinched her skin until she cried out from the pain.

Tessa opened her eyes, looked at her attacker with contempt before she spat in his face.

He sat up, momentarily releasing his grip on her wrists, as he used that hand to deliver a powerful back-hand to her face, then brought it back for good measure.

Throbbing pain exploded through her jaw, as her head twisted, first one way, then the other; something popping or tearing in her neck, sending searing agony down her spine. Her body convulsed with her muted crying, tears falling free and easy onto the sheets below.

When he penetrated her, all other tortuous suffering subsided; only the deprived, burning sting of excruciating degradation thrummed through her entire core.

*

The humiliating ache of her sickening ordeal, hours later, as she lay in a warehouse dormitory filled with other girls, left her feeling weak, disgusted … abnormal.

Tessa lay, on her side, curled into herself, staring at nothing at all, fixated only on how empty and destitute she felt.

Many of the other girls bore similar expressions of desolation; hardly anyone spoke. Some were covered in cuts and bruises, others looked space out, eyes red-rimmed and glazed – high on something that might suppress the reality of their situation. Tessa wondered if it worked; if it might be possible to leave behind all sensibility at the hands of the evil bastards who needed to pay for sex, needed the kick of watching the very life drain from the eyes of their young, innocent victims, as they sullied them in unimaginable ways.

She balked at the thought – flinched internally at the very notion that she might resort to destroying, not only her mind, but her body and soul of her own accord, when these monsters were already hell bent on doing the very same to her.

No – she would not, *could not*, let them take from her anymore than they already had.

Slowly, painfully, she lifted herself from the bed; greeted with questioning, frightened stares from others in the room. On leaden, shaky limbs, she stood, her defiant conviction the only thing giving her the strength she so badly needed.

"What are you doing?"

"Where are you going?"

"Please don't."

"They'll kill us."

Whispers filled the room, the girls scared to shout any louder as they questioned their fellow captive's motives. Tessa only silenced them with a finger to her lips. They might want to stay here, continue to be used, abused and whittled away into nothing, but she did not. She would go out fighting, even if it meant to the death.

Surveying the room, Tessa looked for something she could use as a weapon. Choices were sparse, much like everything else in the warehouse-prison.

"Here." A meek voice spoke up.

Tessa turned to see a small, Asian girl, no older than fourteen, perhaps, brandishing one of the rusted, metal slats from under her bed.

Taking the proffered armament, Tessa thanked the girl, who crawled back between the sheets, maintaining her terrified look, unwilling to participate any further.

She surmised that they would all be a force to be reckoned with, if they just all found the strength to do the same thing – there were at least fifty of them; the numbers were there, but not the will or the desire. Broken and weak, they were resigned to their fate. Tessa wondered how long many of them had been there, forced to give themselves over, in horrific ways, to the vile creatures keeping them captive.

With it still in the back of her mind, Tessa crept toward the only door she could see. Lights shone, dimly, from the other side. The closer she got, the more she could hear the men talking from other positions within the warehouse. Peering through the mucky glass, she could make out at least two in the immediate vicinity. If she positioned herself just right, she could smack them both with the pole in her hands, disorientate them, perhaps, then make a run for it.

She clasped hold of the door knob in her hand, then slowly turned it until the latch clicked back. Pushing, she recoiled quickly when a loud creaking resonated around the room and down the corridor. Wide-eyed, her skin turning cold and clammy, she spotted the two guards turning their head toward the noise.

In a language she didn't understand, one said something to the other, before they both turned, walking briskly toward Tessa.

She backed away from the door, pole brandished in front of her, ready for them to enter.

The first threw open the door.

Tessa swung, smashing the corroded weapon right across the man's bald head. Blood seeped from a hairline laceration and the man pawed at it, his eyes squeezed tight with the pain. The girls began to scream.

The other man barged in, past his friend, shoving him out the way. With evil intend in his eyes, he stomped toward Tessa.

The pole shook in her hand amid the terrified trembles wracking her body. She glanced at it, then at the man before her, then swung again.

Having seen her intent, he grabbed the weapon, yanking it from her hands.

Two girls jumped him, landing on his back, clawing at his face with their nails.

Tessa saw her opportunity. She grabbed the slat from the ground, then ran through the open door, into the faintly-lit corridor, turning in several directions, down other hallways, past other doors. She didn't know the way, began to feel desperate, tired, hopeless.

Then she saw them – yellow, steel doors leading to the outside, to her freedom… to her family.

She burst through them, dropping the slat from her hands.

A tremendous pop echoed through the stillness of the night. Tessa stopped, her body heavy, cold, her head swimming, breath short. The pain in her stomach didn't register, at first. Until she saw the man with the gun, pointed straight at her. He smiled, a sardonic grin, making her to look down.

Her hands were already coated in blood, where she subconsciously clutched at the wound in her belly, seeping dark crimson into the white linen of her nightshirt.

Her knees were the first to give in to the weight bearing them down. Tessa dropped to them, grazing them on the gritted ground beneath her. She fell to the side, her hands trying to stem the flow of blood from her body as the icy coldness spread over her. The surrounding floodlights danced in and out of focus, their brightness dimming gradually. Black stars twinkled, replacing the sparkling white of the ones in the sky above.

Before the blanket of darkness consumed her, a blurred face stood over her, that same grin plastered all over it. His lips moved in speech, but she didn't hear a thing, only the blood rushing through her brain, before that, too, fell silent.

Chapter 1

Two Years Later

It's cold, out in the middle of the North Atlantic Ocean. My body trembles, but I suspect it isn't all down to the chilly bite in the sea air. Adrenaline has a way of keeping me going; but it also finds a way to steady my hand, when the time comes.

I pull up to the side of Marco Ferroli's yacht, tying off my small boat with a length of rope from my bag. Already dressed and ready for the occasion, I stash my bag away, surveying the area, making sure none of his goons are nearby as I board.

Using the shadows, I creep toward the ladders that will take me to main deck. First things first, I need to take care of the men downstairs, in the engine room. The boat is already stationary, but I could do without it pulling off and surprising me while I'm in the middle of doing what I came here to do.

On deck, I can see right through the large, glass doors of Ferroli's living quarters. I peer in at the ruby red and gold extravagance of the main living room, spying a couple of men helping themselves to the liquor at the bar, smoking cigars, laughing, burning holes into the skin of the young girl sat, crying, on one of the barstools.

My blood boils as I watch her porcelain skin glow red, as red as her face as she tries to keep from crying, lest she want another beating; more bruises to match those already circling her sad, watery eyes.

Gritting my teeth together, I tell myself, I'll deal with those men in due course.

Still obscure from the lights inside, I tip-toe my way toward the door that will lead to the engine room, thankful that I'm dressed in black, to blend in against the night sky. I don't know what's going to be on the other side, so, heart in my mouth, I draw a hunting knife from a sheath on my belt, readying myself for what I might face. After a quick glance of my surroundings, I throw the door open, hoping to surprise anyone that might be there.

The stairs leading down are empty. I let out a breath, then descend with trained, silent footsteps, listening out for even the slightest of sounds that might be drowned out by the steady thrum of the engines.

I can hear at least two, male voices, which means I will need to act fast. I pull a second knife from my belt, edging closer to the door that will reveal the two thugs.

Judging from the volume of their voices, I'd say they're pretty close to the door. At least one has his back to me; the one closest to me. The other, I'm not too sure about.

I risk a quick glance, then react within the seconds.

The one with his back to me is, indeed, closest to me. Gliding up to him, I force the length of the first knife into the base of his neck. As the other opens his mouth to say something, I throw my second knife. It buries itself in his larynx, blood oozing from his gapping mouth, over his lips, spilling in ruby-red globules to the floor, before he slumps against the wall. He slides to the floor, his eyes open, lifeless.

I take the weight of the other against my chest, easing him down. He's already dead after having his spinal cord severed. Removing the knife from his neck with a squelch, I wipe it off on the leg of my pants, then retrieve the other from the second man. His body spasms as I pull it out, wiping this one, too, on my leg before sheathing it.

My next target needs to be the idiots circling the decks, so I make my way back upstairs, disappearing into the gloom again.

I spot one of Ferroli's cronies lurking on the deck right in front of me. He's looking out at sea, one hand thumbing the piece strapped to his belt. He's completely unaware, so my heart beat slows a little. Used to this as I am, I can still feel the gushing of my blood as it pounds through me, still partly buzzing from the kills downstairs.

Creeping as carefully as I can, I make my silent way over, dividing my attention between the immediate proximity, and my prey in front of me; with an experienced, expert eye.

His back is to me, when I sneak up on him. Covering his mouth with one hand, I slice the knife in my other, straight into his jugular with practiced finesse. It slides in as though it were a ripe peach; the sound of his flesh tearing not phasing me in the slightest.

Gurgling, the man tries to struggle – but it's futile and ridiculous, while his life ebbs away between my gloved fingers.

He slumps to the deck, and I use my bodyweight to steady him, so he doesn't make a thud when he drops. I need to hide him, for now – I'll dump his body in the sea after I've completed my contract.

Dragging him to a darkened corner, I leave him propped up against the door that leads into the engine room. Having already taken care of Ferroli's pals down there, no-one should be using it any time soon. With the boat still stationary; bobbing on the waves in the middle of nowhere – as per Ferroli's usual request – I know I have time to finish what I've been ordered to do.

If memory serves, there should be another one of Marco's bodyguards on the opposite side of the boat, and if I remember correctly, he's a big bastard – pumped up on steroids, and other, illegal shit. If I'm careful, though, it won't matter – he'll go down just as easily as all the others; with a knife through his throat.

Giving due caution to avoid the lightened areas, I creep my way around to the other side of the yacht, Sure enough, the beefy motherfucker is pacing the deck, and his hand is hovering over the two-way in his back pocket.

I need to be quick; if he radios through and gets no response from any of the other guards, he's gonna be after my ass with more speed than a babysitter's boyfriend when a car pulls up.

I gotta do this, now.

Keeping my eyes on the prize, I stalk closer, knife held out in front of me, the other, half-stretched out to the side, to help me keep my balance.

He turns and spots me, going for his gun on instinct.

Shit! I rush forward and pounce on him, stabbing the blade through the side of his head.

Stumbling, he throws out a meaty fist and batters me in the side of the head.

I loosen my grip on him and we both fall, with the loudest bang in such a quiet, tranquil surrounding. It reverberates across the deck, making the floorboards shudder under the impact.

Rolling forward, I stop myself, looking back at the man. He's clearly dead; brain matter is leaking through the large gash in his head, and his eyes have glazed over already.

On all fours, I pad back over and grab the dagger that fell to the floor, before I throw my head back in the other direction.

There's movement coming from the living quarters; shadows are dancing across the deck and in the windows.

With graceful quickness, I leap up, running for the sliding glass doors with silent steps. But I'm not quick enough. The two guards from the bar run into me, knocking me to the floor. I think they're every bit as dazed as I am, though, since they weren't expecting me so soon, so I use their surprise to my advantage.

Correcting myself, I sweep out one leg, taking away the balance of one of the men. Cursing, he lands on the deck with a thump, while the other launches himself at me.

Lifting my weight with my arms, I use my other leg, aiming high, kicking the advancing moron in the chest. He stumbles back, winded, and I use his moment of unsteadiness to fully stand, retrieving my fallen knife along the way.

The first goon has already pulled himself together; he's going for his gun.

I throw my knife, rejoicing within when it pierces his left eye socket. Blood and viscous matter ooze from the wound before he falls backwards, the gun clattering to the deck.

In those few seconds, I rush the other criminal, grab one of his shoulders, twist my body until I am latched onto his back, then use both arms to break his neck. Dropping like a stone, the fat fucker lands awkwardly on my ankle. I tumble to the side, wincing in pain, clutching the injured article.

"Well, well." Ferroli steps out of the double doors. His white suit is bright in the full moonlight; I'm almost blinded by its brilliance. When he removes his tinted shades – and God knows why he's even wearing them, he adds, "Fallen at the final hurdle, I see."

Sanctimonious asshole. His smile is smug as he goes for the piece nestled at the back of his waistband.

But it's too late.

Swinging my arm around, I level the gun from the deck at his head and shoot. The bullet buries itself between his eyes before he can utter a word – a useless, pointless word, since none of his lackeys are alive to care.

He topples to the floor, dark red seeping from the hole in his forehead. I clamber to my knees, my ankle throbbing, before I set about retrieving proof of my deed.

Something catches my attention. I turn my head to see the wide, petrified eyes of the half-dressed child on Ferroli's couch, her skin still red and burned, tears of terror in her eyes while she watches me.

My heart aches for her – more than she will ever understand – but there's nothing I can do right now. She will be rescued, though – that I can make sure of. I put a bloodied finger in front of my lips, quietening her as I tell her she's safe now.

*

My shaking hands are coated in thick, dark blood. Thank fuck I've been wearing gloves, and thank fuck *they* aren't here, watching while I do this. Mostly, killing comes easy to me – I have no choice, sometimes – but this is an entirely different set of circumstances, and the whole situation makes me nervous. So much depends on this.

The almost-black liquid drips onto the yacht's deck, but I'll be long gone by the time anyone notices. As will all the bodies I've just dumped overboard; eaten by the fish, and God only knows what other creatures, settled within its inky waves.

Patting my pocket, to make sure the evidence of my kill is nestled inside, I remove my sticky gloves, throwing them into the shadowy, choppy sea below. Grabbing my concealed bag from under one of the benches, I pull the black wig off my head, remove the brown contact lenses from my eyes, and shove them all inside, slipping on a wetsuit, and another pair of leather gloves. Glancing at my watch, I nod to myself, noticing I have fifteen more minutes before my escape arrives. Enough time to sink the boat; now that I've ensured I've left no evidence behind – though, I shouldn't have; I'm good at what I do.

Before I set about getting rid of the boat, I cast my gaze out to sea. The girl is disappearing into the gloom of the sea mist, safe on a dinghy with a flare gun, and instructions on when to use it. She'll be rescued, in time.

Retrieving the underwater explosives from my bag, I sit myself on the edge of my boat before diving into the dark waters. I don't need an oxygen kit; this won't take long, I can hold my breath for a good while.

Doing just that, I swim under the boat, planting the device underneath where I know the engine room is. I activate the bomb, then swim back to the surface, releasing my breath, gulping down fresh air as I clamber back aboard before paddling away from Ferroli's yacht.

I grab a flashlight from my holdall, flashing the pre-arranged signal. Another yacht comes into view within moments, and a rope ladder is secured to the side to allow me access. I climb aboard, jumping onto the deck, landing with ease – despite the pain in my ankle – at the helm of the luxury cruiser as it sets sail for land.

Sirus approaches, the glow from the moonlight bouncing off his bald head. “Ferroli?” he asks, with an Italian lilt, one bushy eyebrow raised above his dark glare.

I nod, reaching into my bag once more for the detonator. I press the button. An almighty explosion sends crashing waves in a sizeable radius, rocking the boat we’re on. I pocket the ignition, then turn back to Sirus. “Dead.” Delving into my duffel again, I grab my trophy, slapping the carved-off piece of bloodied scalp into Sirus’s outstretched hand.

With a hitched smile, he says, “Welcome to the Skull Caps.”

While my stomach flips with excited nerves, I keep up appearances, telling him expressionlessly, “I’ll wait to hear that from the horse’s mouth, so to speak.”

He growls and winks at me. “I love your fire.”

Shame; the mere sight of him sickens me.

We’re not too far from land. Though, even the half hour it will take to get back, is half hour more than I’d have liked to have spent on this boat with Sirus, and his bunch of bumbling fuckwits. The way they are leering at me, anyone would think they’d not seen a woman in years … or perhaps, not one older than what they’re used to. Holding my head up, I walk by them all, suppressing a shiver as I feel their eyes all over me, though, they don’t say anything. *That’s right, boys, I’m likely to bite back.*

“Whose idea was it to have women in the Skull Caps?”

There’s always one that thinks his balls are bigger than everyone else’s.

“What’s wrong?” I ask, turning to face the gap-toothed moron who opened his mouth. “Do real women intimidate you?” He glowers at me, but I don’t stop there. “Or is it that they've enough wits about them to understand what an ugly, inbred, simpleminded prick you are?"

He pulls a knife from somewhere on his person.

"Oh." I take a step back. "It's all of the above?"

I'm expecting it when he rushes me, clumsily handling a weapon he clearly has no idea how to use properly.

Side-stepping him, so that his outstretched arm is in front of me, I grab his limb with one hand, then snap it at the elbow with the other. The knife clatters to the deck as he screams out in pain, tumbling, awkwardly to his knees. Reaching down, I pick up the blade, toying with it in my hands. "Nice piece of equipment." I walked toward him, and he has the decency to look momentarily frightened, before I plunge the knife into his thigh.

His screams pierce the still night, joined by the odd chuckle, or insult thrown his way by the rest of the guys on board.

"In answer to your question," I tell him, dropping to one knee in front of him, as he clutches the area of his leg around the knife blade, "is that some women are just better at handling weapons, than the men who own them." My slightly-intentional innuendo is met with more laughter as I stand and walk away.

*

Back on dry land, we wait at the docks for the limo to show. My nerves are beginning to get the better of me at the anticipation of sitting down in front of the boss. I need him to sign off on my acceptance into the Skull Caps. They're also a little shot to shit because I have wanted to kill this man for a long, long time, but I need to wait; there's too much more at stake if I just off him tonight. *My* boss has a lot riding on me getting on their good side. It's an inconvenience for me, but not one I can do anything about, at the moment.

Soon enough, headlights penetrate the approaching dawn, heading straight for us. The ridiculously pretentious car pulls up in front of us. A handsome, olive-skinned man with chiselled good looks and dark hair steps out. He's wearing a black suit, with a blue tie that matches the azure tones of his eyes. When he sees me, he smiles a dazzling smile, full of pearly-white teeth and luscious, pink lips.

"Asha," he purrs, holding out his hand for me to shake, which I do. "I trust the contract was carried out."

"She did well, boss." Sirus slides up beside me, his arm brushing the side of my ass.

I glare daggers at him, moving slightly away, so as to not risk hurling my guts up all over Dieter Pérez's expensive attire.

He must find it hilarious, as he's looking at me, grinning like a Cheshire Cat, while he hands Dieter the evidence of my completed mission.

The mob boss turns it over in his hands, staining them with the remnants of dried blood and matted hair.

“That enough for you?” I know I’m pushing my luck, talking to Dieter so coldly. Despite his good looks, he’s a hard bastard, but he also respects professional tenacity.

With a nod, he tells me, “It’s enough. Welcome to my family, Asha.”

My elation is short-lived, when, turning his attention away from me, Dieter motions, with a click of his fingers, toward the idling limo. Two men step out either side; one of them is hauling another out with him, amid protests and a struggle. The other goes around the other side to help. Between them both, they bring the terrified-looking Hispanic man closer to Dieter and the rest of us.

“B-boss, p-please. It wasn’t me, I s-swear.” He’s rambling, sweat pouring from his brow, down his ashen, yet bloodied and bruised face.

Dieter doesn't seem to care. He looks at the man, then nods to his two gorillas.

They haul him over to some low scaffolding, throwing a rope over the top pole, securing it in place before looping the end.

"Wait, please." The guy is crying now, his tears mingling with the grime already coating his face.

No-one listens; no-one cares.

While the man continues to plead his innocence over an unknown fuck up, he is helped onto a crate that's been placed underneath the noose, before the rope is strung around his neck, tight.

"You shouldn't have betrayed me." It's the only thing Dieter utters, before he kicks the box from beneath the man's feet.

I look on, impassive, yet fraught with dread on the inside, as the man digs at the rope in his neck, his legs dancing erratically below him.

His face bloats, likely because of the rope cutting into his neck as he battles with it. Raised, red scratches mar his pale neck, made all the more prominent the bluer his lips turn. His eyes bulge one last time, as he lets out his final breathe, then the struggling ceases.

Dieter turns away, ordering his men to cut down the body, dump it in the ocean.

“Boss?” Sirus sidles up to Dieter. “We had a bit of an issue on board. Your man, here,” he tells him, pointing at the guy with the knife in his leg, “tried to take out one of our own.” He nods his head in my direction.

“I wouldn’t go that far.” I turn my own attention toward the mob boss, careful to keep any trepidation from my voice. “Technically, I wasn’t part of the family then, and, he couldn’t have hit a stationary car with a monster truck, the way he was coming at me.”

Nostrils flaring, Dieter draws his top lip between his teeth. “Regardless, I won’t tolerate insubordination, not from anyone.” He gives Sirus the nod.

The tall, bald man draws a silenced pistol from his belt, turns to face his intended victim, and shoots him in the chest.

The man doesn't die instantly. He crumples, in a heap, to the floor, clutching his injury, blood dribbling from between his paling lips.

What a way to make a man suffer. I almost feel sorry for him, as I watch his prolonged agony. Walking toward Sirus, I take the gun from his hand, point it at the man and shoot, planting one between his eyes.

"He might have been as asshole." I hand Sirus his weapon back. "But there's no need to join him." Devoid of any emotion, I walk back over to Dieter. "I'd already made him suffer," I tell him, heading toward the limo.

Before I clamber inside, I hear Dieter murmur his approval with an almost animalistic growl.

He and Sirus follow me into the limo, taking their seats. The mob boss opens the mini bar, then pours three, ample-sized measures of amber liquid. He hands one to Sirus, then to me, before gulping back his own. “We’re gonna have some fun, you and I.” He smiles, a saccharin-sweet expression that gives me butterflies in my stomach.

I nod my apparent approval, before I down the glass of bourbon in one shot, trying, desperately, to keep my hands from shaking with fearful exhilaration.

Chapter 2

My hotel room is cold when I enter, despite the soaring temperatures outside. I dump my bag by the side of the bed, turn the AC off and strip down for a shower, throwing my jeans and tank top on top of the desk, beneath the window in the room.

It's bright outside, no clouds in the sky, as I look out and admire the view of the sea. If only I could appreciate it's full worth, and not the notion it now holds for me.

I can only hazard a guess as to where Ferroli's watery grave now lies; my stomach churns at the thought of what that man stood for, what he did, how many lives he ruined. Ferroli isn't… wasn't, a good man, not in any way, shape or form. I've done the streets, and poor, unsuspecting teen girls a favor getting rid of him – despite the reasons behind it. I don't feel guilty in the slightest, I only feel that his death should have come about a lot sooner.

Padding into the bathroom, I turn the shower faucet on, testing the temperature before deciding I want it scalding hot. I need to scrub my skin until it's burning, red raw. Only then, will I feel clean again.

I stand in front of the mirror, examining my appearance. I'm tired; dark circles surround my baby blue eyes, which, over the years, have lost some of their lustre. They stare back at me, vacant, jaded, wondering who the hell I am anymore.

Pushing my dark blonde hair behind my ears, I drag my gaze down the top half of my body, eyeing up the multitude of scars; some big, some small, some with more significance than others. I still have the lean body of a thirty-four-year-old, but the real damage is what's been done on the inside. My heart has aged beyond its years. I may not look as weary as I feel inwardly, but my mind and soul would tell you a completely different story.

Do I regret some of my life choices? Yeah, sure I do. Do I feel like I had a choice? Not always. Philosophers would argue that we all have choices, but really, some of those choices would carry more consequences and regrets than others. I suppose it's still a choice, at the end of the day, but who ultimately decides whether it's the right or the wrong one?

Contemplations aside, I make my way back into my room. Sitting myself at the desk, I open the lid of my laptop. The previous night, I did a little research on Ferroli. I always knew of his extra-curricular proclivities, but I wanted to research more about his movements, lifestyle, who his top men were. Likely, one of those buffoons will now take top spot, so, while I've got rid of one foul pimple on the face of this earth, another would pop up in its place.

The images on my screen come into focus – plans of the same model of yacht Ferroli once owned, news articles on the accomplishments of his men; names omitted, of course, but I know enough about them to know which ones were responsible for what crimes, and which ones he, ultimately, kept close as a reward for their misdeeds.

Like I said before, I'm good at what I do.

I close down all the windows, deleting my search history after. It won't completely erase all traces of my prying into their affairs, but it'll do for the time being. Once done, I grab my phone from my bag, placing a call to my boss.

"Warren," the voice on the other end states.

"I'm in." We forgo the usual pleasantries, I just want to get straight to the point, and straight off the phone. The less time I spend on it, the less suspicious I look if someone catches me. "I'll update you again in a few hours."

"Woah, hold on a minute." Warren's tone loses some of the professionalism. "I haven't heard from you in over forty-eight hours; what's new?"

Releasing an impatient breath, I tell him, "This isn't a social call. If there was anything new, I'd have told you."

"You might be working with hardened criminals right now, but I'm still your boss; don't talk to me like a prick, understood?" The edge returns to his words. "I need to know you're safe at all times, so shoot me if part of wanting that knowledge is because I give a shit what happens to you." His voice softens a little, but still carries a tense undertone. "What did you have to do?"

"Kill some people." I'm getting increasingly impatient of this conversation.

"This job is changing you."

"Oh, get fucked, Tony. What did you expect? I'm running with the very scum that I despise. It might be my job, but you know how I feel about getting involved with them. They're into more than just drugs, you know." I lay my head in my free hand, massaging the ache beginning to settle there. "Anyway, it's not like they didn't deserve it."

"Get your head outta your ass, I'm only interested in the drugs. Screw the rest of what they're into … no pun intended." I can hear the smile in his words. "That's not our concern."

"Asshole, you're not funny. If we can kill two birds, and all that."

"Not on my dime, sweetheart. Get your claws into the drugs, stay outta everything else." He pauses for effect. "And for crying out loud, try not to kill any more mob bosses."

He knows. "If you knew, why did you ask?"

"Word travels. And we found your little teen beauty floating in the deep blue."

At least I did that right. I managed to instruct the girl to fire the flare just when I knew patrols would be around to rescue her. Seems word *does* get around. "I'm not apologising for that, nor for anything else. They deserved to die; she didn't."

Flicking through some crap on my laptop, hoping to stem the boredom of going over the same shit, I sit upright when I open my surveillance feed. "I gotta go," I tell Warren, "Rico is here."

"You be careful around him; he's dodgy as fuck."

"Aren't we all, one way or another? And besides, nothing is going on. He's my contact, that's all."

"Who you trying to justify yourself to?"

"Fuck you, Tony." I hang up the call, then stash my phone and laptop away.

A knock echoes from the door and I run to grab a towel from the bathroom rail, wrapping myself in it before securing the loose end between my breasts.

"Asha?"

I stop, fingers hovering over the door handle. My heart flutters and I swallow past my dry throat. Against my better judgement, I throw the door open, releasing a deep breath before his exotic, handsome features appear before me.

His smile sends butterflies coursing through me, when he pulls me into a tight embrace.

"You did it." He kisses my lips. "You're one of us, now."

Ever since I'd been trying to get into the Skull Caps, over a year ago, Rico and I *have* developed an intimate relationship. He's Dieter's right-hand man, so our fucking one another is no secret among the crew. I, however, am in two minds about it, but it's all part and parcel – or so I tell myself.

He's different to the rest of Dieter's men – and Dieter himself. He's sweet and caring, and hot as sin. He sets my pulse racing like no other man has, so much so, that I can't help myself around him.

He might be a bad boy, but he's not involved in *all* the shit I know the mob boss is. I've done my homework – he keeps himself relatively off the radar.

I'm trying to justify my being with him – because it goes against everything I stand for, everything I've worked for. It compromises my position, but I can't stop myself.

Cupping my ass cheeks in his large, warm hands, he hoists me up, and I circle my legs around his waist; the towel slipping from me. He growls, burying his head in my tits, kicking the door closed before throwing me on the bed.

Crawling backward, I giggle a delighted sound, spreading my legs for him. He loves to watch me tease myself, so, I slide one hand down my thigh, the other down my stomach; slow, leaning my head back, arching my hips, giving myself goosebumps. I reach my mound and dip between, rubbing my clit. "You want this, baby?" I purr, licking my dry lips, as I lift my head to look at him.

"Fuck, yes," he groans, adjusting the sizeable bulge in his jeans, while he stares at me with unabashed lust, smirking, nostrils flaring like he wants to eat me alive.

He moves forward, but I shake my finger at him. "Nah ah, not yet, stud." I want to have a little fun with him first.

Tracing my hands around my thighs, I further part my legs, exposing the silky lips of my moist, shaven pussy. Bringing my hand to my face, I dip two fingers into my mouth, trailing them over my tits, down my stomach and over my aching clit. With my other hand, I knead my breast, tweaking my nipple.

Rico tears his jeans and shirt off, then grips the base of his long, thick cock. “Fuck, babe, you are so damn sexy.”

I bite my bottom lip. “Mmm, imagine your tongue right here.” I circle my throbbing bud, then dip two fingers inside my hot, wet entrance. “Let me feel you, Rico. Run your tongue across my pussy.”

“*My* pussy,” he growls, while he drops in front of me.

He grabs my thighs in his large hands and dips down, tugging me closer before gliding his tongue from my ass crack to my clit.

I moan out loud, arching my hips into him. “Oh, yes. Right there.” My words are drawn out, barely audible, such is the effect his tongue has on me. Already my legs are shaking.

"You taste so fuckin' sweet." He plunges his tongue deep inside me, flicking the tip up, grazing my sweet spot, sending my body into delicious spasms with every glance.

Groans rumble in my chest, and I part my still-dry lips, leaning my head back, closing my eyes. I grab both breasts and pull on my stiffened nipples; electrifying currents shooting through my body, exploding warm and inviting in my core.

"Fuck me," I breathe.

Rico climbs onto the bed, hovering over me, his deliciously hazel eyes centred on mine, with one hand at the side of my face while the other positions his dick at my slick pussy. "You want this in you?" He teases my opening with the tip of his swollen head, rubbing up and down my pulsing slit.

Arching my hips into him, we both gasp when the tip of his cock enters me. I hook a leg around his ass and draw him in, hard.

Air rushes from my lungs, explodes from my lips in loud moans when he thrusts deep, filling me with his length.

"Fuck, Asha," he grunts, grabbing the back of my head, driving further into me.

I rake my nails across his back and lift myself up, burying my face in his shoulder, biting down on the soft flesh, trying to muffle my delirious cries, while I lift my hips to his rhythm.

Grabbing hold around my waist, he hauls me up, throwing my legs either side of his.

I lean back on my palms, raising my hips, over and over, taking in every exquisite inch of his engorged cock. It strokes the inside of me, rubs off every inch of my greedy pussy while I tightened myself around him.

Pulling me forward, he puts my arms around his neck and captures my lips with his. He bounces me off his shaft, driving into me balls-deep, the wiry texture of his pubic hair rubbing against my responsive clit.

Sweat pours from his hardened body, glistening in the curves of his sculpted abs, as he pounds into me with relentless thrusts.

I bite his lip, drawing blood. “Harder, Rico. Make me cum; I’m so close.”

Rising to his knees, he holds on to me, while he powers in hard, fast.

I scream out his name, feeling him swell inside me, grinding against the tight walls of my trembling sex.

I thumb my clit when he pushes into me and cry out, gushing around his cock.

He lets loose a feral sound, bursting inside me, filling me with hot cum, while I tighten around him, milking him of his release, relishing the crashing waves of my delectable climax as they sweep through me.

We fall either side of one another, spent and breathing heavy. Rico slides his arm across my chest, grazing my nipples, sending quick bursts of tingling heat to my quivering core, making me shudder beneath him, smiling and content, my eyes closed.

Before long, Rico's soft breathing evens out, and I allow satiated bliss to take over me.

Chapter 3

Lying on my back, I stare at the ceiling fan going around and around, listening to the splashing of the shower I left on earlier.

I've been awake for some time, swamped by contemplation, and perhaps, somewhere in all this mess, the smallest of regrets. I've done some shitty things in my life to get what I want, but none have involved such cold-blooded murder. Don't get me wrong, though, I still don't feel guilty that they're dead; nothing has ever consumed me as completely as extracting my revenge for what has been done to my family, and I will do whatever it takes to get to those responsible. *Whatever it takes.*

Rico stirs beside me, his arm over my chest. Soft snores escape his slightly-parted lips and I stare at his handsome face. *Are you one of my regrets?* I worry I've gotten in too deep, but something about him took my breath away the very moment I sank behind the warm depths of his caramel eyes. Of all the things I thought I could avoid, getting involved with the enemy is right up there.

Feelings and emotions have eluded me for a long time, but he awoke something in me and I haven't the energy to fight it off. I don't want to.

Careful not to wake him, I slide from under Rico's hold and climb out of bed. My bag lies beneath the open window and, stealing one last look at Rico, I quickly grab one of the phones from the side pocket, then tiptoe to the bathroom and lock myself in. It's risky, but I have little choice.

Using the sound of the shower to drown out any other, I sit on the side of the bath and type in the passcode to unlock my phone. I find the number I need, and fire off a quick message:

JUST CHECKING IN, AS PER YOUR REQUEST… ONLY NEWS IS THAT I'M HUNGRY AND ABOUT TO SHOWER. WILL UPDATE IN 24 HOURS

It's petty, I know, but I couldn't give a shit; Warren deserves it.

Stripping off, I slip my phone inside the seam of my bra meant for padding, and fold it into the rest of my clothes.

After a quick shower, I pad back through to the bedroom; naked. Rico is still out cold and I dump my phone back in my bag, fish out a gun-cleaning kit, and then zip up the pocket before throwing it out of sight. My Glock is on the table, and I grab it, sitting myself down to take it apart. With due care, I lavish the kind of respect and attention reserved for deadly weapons on my baby.

"Do you realise how hot you look right now?"

Hearing Rico's sleepy drone, I look up, smiling. His dark hair is a sexy, dishevelled mess, falling over his deep, brown eyes.

"Girl, you sure know how to handle your weapon. Come on over here and take care of your man's." He grabs his dick, flicking his tongue over his top lip when he winks at me.

On the floor, Rico's jeans start ringing. Cursing, he reaches into the pocket and pulls out his phone with an irritated scowl.

"What now? ... Fine, be there in twenty." Hanging up, he tosses the phone on the bed and gets up. "I gotta scoot, baby. Duty calls. To be continued?"

I smile, nodding, the disappointment likely etched into my features, since Rico keeps apologising, kissing me lightly all over my face. "You better go," I tell him, with a soft smile, "or you're gonna get into trouble for being late." My grin widens when I look at him from under my lashes. "And tell Dieter I want in on the next one."

Growling at me, he kisses me once more, then leaves.

I look at my phone – the one I can have out on the display; the one that Dieter gave me some months ago – and wonder, when will he call me to get in on his jobs. I'm in, now; I've definitely proved my worth to him, so I'm hoping it's only a matter of time. I would have pushed Rico to take me this morning, but I have something I need to do today.

Dressing quickly, I grab my gun from the table, then delve into my bag for a few other bits I will need, before I make way out of the hotel, and onto the hot, sticky Miami streets.

The snooker hall I'm heading toward, is set in the back-alley of nowhere, the entryway surrounded by overflowing trash cans and God only knows what else. I've seen hookers bring their punters up here, so I tread carefully, not wanting to fall flat on my ass in this disease-infested dump. I detest coming here, but I need some information, and this kind of place houses the sort of low-life inbreeds I need that information from.

Turning my nose up, I push open the door to the dive bar, strolling in, trying not to breathe in too much of the smell of cigarettes and whiskey. I'm met with curious stares, from what I can only imagine are the regulars. They glare at me over their murky-stained glasses of liquor.

I walk up to the bar. "I'm here to see Bruno; he's expecting me."

The bartender only points his finger to the ceiling, then casts a cursory glance toward a set of stairs at the back of the room.

Thanking him, I make my way up.

The corridor at the top of the stairs leads to one door, which is usually locked. Bruno Martinez isn't a pleasant man, and he doesn't like unwanted, unwelcome guests. I lied to the bartender; Bruno isn't exactly expecting me, but I need to see him, I don't have the patience to wait.

Knocking on the door, I wait until I hear footsteps approaching from the other side.

"Yeah? Who is it?" The voice is gruff, with an air of impatience.

"Asha. I need to see Bruno."

I'm met with stony silence for long, frustrating moments. Opening my mouth to speak again, I quickly shut it when the door opens.

"Fuck you want?" Bruno is stood before me, a cigarette balancing precariously between his thick lips.

"Can I come in?"

The olive-skinned Italian steps to the side, allowing me entry.

As I pass him, he grabs hold of my hair, yanking my head back. I yell, more in surprise, than pain. "What the hell?"

"What have you been told about turning up here, unannounced?" He tugs my hair further toward him.

“I’ve got what you asked for.” Twisting, I try to loosen some of the grip he has, I’m starting to feel some of my hair pull from the roots. “And I need more information. I’m willing to pay double.”

Knowing how greedy Bruno is, I'm not surprised that his hold on me loosens when I tell him that. He lets me go, but shoves me forward with his palm to the middle of my back.

"This had better be good," he grunts, leading me to a vacant table by one of the blind-covered windows. The slats are open, so the blazing sunlight is pouring in.

I avoid touching the table as I sit, fearing it might sear my skin, such is the intensity of the heat coming from it. I'm sure I can detect a faint smell of burning wood, but I don't say anything – it's not my problem. I'm here for one thing, and one thing only. "I need some names from you." I look at Bruno, square in the eye – he reacts better to eye contact, doesn't feel like you're trying to hide something from it and, while I kinda am, I know how to make it look inconspicuous.

"What you need, is to hand me over payment for the last lot of information you got from me." Bruno has a look of distaste in his eyes; I'm sure he doesn't like me, but I can give him what he's after, so he looks the other way, begrudgingly.

Sliding a hand into my bra, I pull three small packs of white powder from the seam. Handing it over to Bruno, I remind him, "That's grade A, *quality* shit."

Dipping his finger into the powder, he tells me, "I'll be the judge of that," before wiping some on his teeth. His eyes light up, widening as he sits quite still.

I can only assume he's happy with the product when he grins. "Good enough?"

"Good enough. Now," he continues, stowing away the baggies, "what is it you're after this time?"

Fishing a piece of paper from the pocket of my jeans, I slide it across the table toward him. "I need to know where these girls are now." My stomach is in knots, I know this is a long-shot; most of the girls on my list are probably dead by now, but I have to try. "I'll get you six bags for this information."

Bruno stares at my list, his face impassive as he strokes his goatee. “You’ll get me ten,” he finally informs me.

“Ten?” That’s ridiculous, and would be far too expensive if I weren’t desperate.

Clicking his fingers, Bruno looks first to my left, and then to my right, before two of his heavies place a meaty hand on either of my shoulders. “Is that going to be a problem, Asha? I’d hate to think, after everything you’ve done for me so far, we’d have to *part ways* over a measly four extra bags.”

Asshole. He knows he has me backed into a corner, and I know what he means by *part ways.* It wouldn’t be a pleasant parting; more bloody and death-like. I have no choice. “Ten it is.” I eye up each of his muscle, my raised brow insisting that they remove their hands; we’re good here.

I turn my attention back to Bruno. “Two weeks?” Surely that’s plenty of time, it’s time I’m gonna need to get what he wants.

"One." He holds up a finger. "I need more of this." He pats the pocket he put the coke in, smiling. "And I don't wanna hear any protests. One week, or my guys come looking for you, and if that happens, they're not gonna go easy on you for time wasted."

I can't argue with him, he could have me killed in the blink of an eye. He's the only one I know – the only one who cares less enough to help me – that can get me the information I so badly need. I have no choice. Ten bags, one week – this should be fun.

*

Closing my hotel room door behind, I meander over to the bed, throwing myself on it, face first. This whole situation sucks. I need to get my hands on some serious cash to get what Bruno is asking of me. Hauling myself up, I grab my phone from the nightstand, open my phonebook and place a call.

Rico answers almost immediately.

"When will Dieter let me in on his deals? I think I've proved myself to him, don't you?"

"Good afternoon to you, too, babe."

I've got no time for chitchat, but I could do without him getting suspicious from any urgency in my voice. "Come on, babe, I'm going stir crazy over here. I've been killing myself to join for ages, now. I want some of the action." I soften my tone, almost sounding whiny. Better that, than tipping anyone off to the real reason I need these jobs.

"You're right. Girl, you are one bad-ass bitch." He blows me a kiss down the phone. "Come over now. I'll talk him into finding you something on this job."

My heart hammers against my chest, but I keep my demeanor rigid, nodding, then voicing my acceptance to Rico. This is the moment I've worked so hard for – have literally killed for – to get close; this *will* kill two birds.

Once I get my money from Dieter for this job, I can get Bruno's drugs, and he can give me the whereabouts of the girls I need to find; Dieter's girls.

Chapter 4

Dieter's terracotta, Spanish-style villa is huge; and it's not surprising given how much money he earns from dealing drugs and trafficking frightened, young women – girls, even. He's got quite the reputation, alongside a tremendous fear factor because he doesn't care who he hurts, maims or kills. I'll admit, he even scares me. But I have to put that aside, dig deep for my lady balls of steel.

The taxi pulls up outside his countryside mansion and get out of the car, where Rico meets me before we head up the ornate stone steps leading to a huge, oak door. I swallow hard when Rico pushes it open and walks right in. Following him, I'm in awe at the lavish luxury dripping from every square inch of the place.

Rico grabs my hand, intertwining his fingers with mine, and walks me through the parlor to the vast kitchen.

Dieter is sat at the head of a large workstation, amid plumes of cloying cigar smoke. The stench of marijuana clings to the atmosphere, making me want to cough. Four of Dieter's goons – Sirus being one of them – loiter around him, chatting in animated tones, puffing on half-spent joints.

Sirus notices me first, then my hand enveloped in Rico's. He scowls, but says nothing, instead returning his attention to Dieter and clearing his throat.

The mob boss looks up. "Asha?" He casts Rico an inquisitive raised brow and unease settles in the pit of my stomach.

"It's about time Asha got involved, D. She's proved herself; she's been accepted."

Dieter's jaw tenses and he grinds his teeth. "Just because you're fucking, doesn't make it your call. *I* decide when someone's ready; not you." His voice is low and menacing, eyes squinted, swapping his gaze between the two of us.

"Sorry, boss." Rico remains upright, rigid, staring at the hardened gangster.

Dieter turns to me. “As it happens, I think you are ready. You may stay.” He shoots Rico one more warning glance, then nods for us to sit.

Around the table, there’s a litter of paperwork, schematics, print-outs, all kinds of stuff I don’t fully recognise. Though, I do see maps of the marina, radar scans and other such stuff to suggest Dieter’s expecting something to arrive by sea.

“The drop will come in here, so I figure Wicks will have men here, here and here, minimum.” Dieter points to areas on the map likely to be guarded as Wicks’s shipment of drugs comes into the country.

He’s mistaken. “I disagree.” It’s ballsy, but I need these guys to know – to think – I’m all about helping them. I can feel several of the men glaring daggers at me, so I elaborate. “You’re right to suggest here, but if it were my shipment coming in, I’d have men stationed somewhere less obvious.” I study the maps for precious seconds. “They’ve been hit before; they’ll be expecting a play to be made again; though they might not suspect who by. I'd put guys here and here." I point to more secluded spots along the beachfront. "These areas are covered by rock formations, perfect for staying hidden, and especially if they have men in plain sight as decoys. Wicks doesn't care who of his men dies; they're all expendable in his eyes." I risk a glance up, expecting to see a gun pointed at my face.

I'm certain it's surprise mingled with impression etched into Dieter's face. "I was right; you are ready." He looks back at the map. "I'll take your advice, but I still want the other areas covered, too. We can't be too sure."

Rico is grinning at me like a buffoon, quite pleased that his girl has a brain for strategy, it would seem. He does look cute, though, so I return his smile with a hitched one of my own, winking at him for good measure.

A clashing behind startles me, and I twist my head toward the commotion, trying to remain unperturbed.

"What the fuck, Jimmy?" Dieter stands, slamming his hand on the worktop.

Jimmy fumbles with the trays and cutlery he's knocked over before righting himself, twitching, shaking, sweating like a beast in a bear trap.

"B-boss, she got away; gave us the slip." His words are hurried and slurred – the dozy bastard's high as fuck. "I don't even know how; she was dosed up." Jimmy's face pales and he wrings his hands in front of him, surveying the room, his face growing redder by the second as he hopes his story is believable.

It isn't.

Taking a slow walk toward Jimmy, Dieter growls. "You wanna know why she got away, asshole?" Dieter gets in Jimmy's face, and the frightened criminal steps back, swallowing hard. "Because you're off your fuckin' tits again." He slaps Jimmy around the head. "I warned you. I told you what would happen if you let another girl slip."

"P-please, boss. Please d-don't." He backs up further, into the patio doors, fumbling for the handle, his face paling further, visible beads of sweat dripping down his forehead.

A sickness swirls in my stomach when Dieter pulls a gun from the waistband of his trousers, but I remain quiet, hiding my sweaty palms between my legs.

The mob boss puts the barrel against Jimmy's head, and shoots.

The sound echoes around the large room and rings through my ears. Blood and brain matter coat the patio doors, and a couple of the nearby guys, as Jimmy drops like a sack of shit.

I don't flinch – I can't afford to. They have to keep thinking I'm a hardened gang-runner. If they find out the truth, it'll be my brains decorating Dieter's kitchen next.

"Maz, clean this shit up and get rid of the body."

The guy to my left – who I know only as Mario – moves away to do the boss's bidding.

I've seen the aftermath of shootings before; I'm no stranger to blood and violence. But this is a first – watching someone's brains blown into mush from such close proximity, hearing the splatter as large, dark globs of thick gore hit the glass before sliding down. I have to suck it up, though. Too much depends on me not losing my shit.

Dieter calmly retakes his position at the table, not even looking back at the mess that once was Jimmy. His face is nonchalant, he's not even broke a sweat as he resumes discussions of tonight's job.

He unnerves me; I'm not ashamed to say. His whole presence is intimidating without even trying to be. This is a man who sliced his own brother's throat because he got too careless with money that didn't belong to him. Such is life when you're hooked on gambling, owe money to people who, believe it or not, will kill for a lot less than Dieter Pérez.

*

Mario didn't relish the fact that he'd been told to clean up the remains of Jimmy's head from the kitchen doorway.

Now, sat back at the table, he looks sick – his skin is green, his eyes are a little dull, mouth clamped shut as though he might blow chunks if he dares open it. He's not looking favorably at Dieter, either, as the mob boss continues to discuss the drug heist.

Such is life, I'm afraid.

"We'll continue this later." Dieter's smooth voice distracts me from my musings, while he slides back on his chair. "I think we all need a little downtime before the job." He snaps his fingers before a hoard of busty women in too-small bikinis saunter, giggling, into the kitchen from another room.

The bimbos each go to one of the criminals, litter kisses on their faces as they drag them outside to the large pool.

One tries her luck with Rico, shoving her ample – clearly fake – breasts in his face. Lashing out my hand, I grab her nipple, twisting it before it can do any damage as it heads towards Rico's face. "Get your fucking hands, and your plastic tits away from my man, before I rip this thing off and choke you with it."

The dozy bitch squeals like a tied-up hog – very ladylike, trying to swat my hand away like it's a fly on shit.

I squeeze one last time, releasing her, pushing her back a little as I do, before she runs off toward the pool, diving in, wetting her face to cover up the tears I saw in the corners of her eyes.

Without a word, Rico gets up – I hope he isn't mad at me; I'm not usually that possessive. I don't think he is, though; he has a lust-fuelled glint in his hooded eyes. Grabbing my hand, he hauls me off the chair, dragging me behind him as I right myself from the sudden onslaught of his need to take me away from the noise outside.

He leads me upstairs, into one of the many plush bedrooms I imagine are used for guests. There's a familiar scent lingering in the air, something I can't quite put my finger on. It's soon forgotten as I take in the gorgeous pale blue of the walls, complimented with white wood décor. In the centre, stands a large, white, four-poster bed. Rico throws off the pale, lace bedding before lowering me down onto the comfortable mattress beneath him.

Shimmying further up, I allow him space to climb on after me. His hungry smile is making me weak at the knees; I can't help but return it, closing my eyes as he showers my neck with light, fluttery kisses.

My body breaks out in goosebumps under his delicate, yet delectable assault. I'm high on him, delirious, moaning softly when he lifts up my tank top, runs his lips across my navel, up, higher, moving the material as he goes. When he reaches my nipple, swipes his tongue across the hardened bud, I groan out loud, fisting his hair, coaxing him into sucking me hard.

He obliges, taking more than enough into his mouth, sucking, licking, teasing me until the butterflies in my stomach move their provocative dance lower and lower, leaving a simmering trail of desire in their wake.

I need more.

Ripping off my top, I arch my back, cursing with delight when Rico takes my other nipple between his teeth.

His hands stroke their way down my stomach; a whispered touch, until he reaches the waistband of my jeans. With a deft swiftness, he has them undone, leaving him room to ease his hand inside.

I'm not wearing any panties.

Rico growls his approval, before two of his fingers find my aching clit. I'm already wet, and he uses my own juices as a lubricant to add further friction as he rubs.

Spasms take over me, my legs quiver with each stroke.

He's relentless; gaining speed the more my body quakes. He moves his body up mine, sucking my bottom lip between his teeth, as he pushes two fingers deep inside me, brushing his thumb across my swollen bud.

The deeper he goes, the thirstier I become for release. My feet and fingers tingle, head swimming with an amalgamation of colors, patterns and white stars.

When he stops, I cry out. *No, no, no*, what is he doing? I am so close.

"Rico?" my pleading voice is husky, throat dry. "Why have you stopped?" Raising myself up on my elbows, my stomach flips at the look of smug pleasure on his face, brow raised. If he wants to play games, I'm all for it.

Shifting further up the bed, I free myself from underneath him. He's curious as to what I'm going to do; he's looking at me with the unasked question behind his gaze.

I beckon him closer with my finger, to which he readily obliges. Using my advantage, I grab his shoulders, flipping him over, so that he is beneath me. He likes it; his nostrils flare when his jaw tightens, so I pout at him, widening my eyes with mock pity while he is positioned at my mercy.

With quick proficiency, I tug off his pants, leaving him exposed to me. It's a sight I will never tire of. His enlarged length bobs in front of me, eager to feel the silky strokes of my tongue up and down the shaft. I am more than willing to please.

Lowering my head, using one hand to grip the base of his cock, I lavish my tongue across the tip, flicking up, down, side-to-side, lapping up the small dribbles of pre-cum that seep from his head. My tongue tingles with the taste, my body yearning for more.

He wants more, too; he's moving his hips in rhythm with my mouth, desperate for me to close my lips around his entirety.

I make him wait, instead, teasing further, gliding my tongue from his balls, all the way up, with languid, enticing caresses, making him pulsate against my lips.

He hisses my name between gritted teeth.

I take him whole, sliding his wide cock to the back of my throat, over and over, using one hand to pump his length between my lips. He curses when my free hand massages his swollen balls. He throbs in my mouth; I love the feeling, knowing that I am the reason he is close to climax. It turns me on all the more, making me crave the sweet swell of him between my legs.

Releasing his dick from both mouth and hand, I am somewhat self-satisfied when he groans his displeasure, begging me not to stop.

"I want to cum in your mouth," he moans, thrusting his hips toward me.

Ignoring his pleas, I yank off my jeans, throwing them to the floor before I straddle him.

His erection tickles my already sensitive clit, making my pussy quake for the feel of him deep within me.

Lowering myself, I take a firm grip of his cock, gliding it back and forth across my smooth folds, coating him with my excitement, dipping the tip inside my wet entrance once or twice, enough to make him moan louder. With each delicate movement, my lips part further, letting out soft groans of rapturous bliss.

Not able to take much more, I slam myself down on him, crying out with both pleasure and pain as I take every inch of him, deep.

“Fuck,” Rico lets out, on a heavy breath.

Rocking my hips, my breath comes out in fervent pants when Rico moves his hips in sync with mine. I feel him in places never felt before, as he rocks back and forth, his beautifully magnified cock grinding against the tightening walls of my core.

I reach down between my legs, strumming my clit with two fingers, ready – desperate – to lose myself inside the unstable, unbridled pinnacle of euphoria I can feel washing over me, as volatile as a storm at sea.

When it hits, burning a path as hot as a forest fire, I scream out Rico's name, trying, with everything in me to stay upright, to ride out each crashing wave as it gushes through me. My nails dig into the muscled flesh of Rico's chest, deep enough to draw blood.

When he erupts inside me, I fall forward, unable to hold myself up any longer. My body's trembling, I can't control it.

"Asha?"

I barely register when Rico murmurs my name against my ear. It sends tingles down my spine, and all I can do is moan an almost insensible response.

With such gentleness, he moves me off him, laying me at his side, letting me curl into his burly body, as mine gives up the last of my strength.

Chapter 5

The light outside is fading, by the time I open my eyes. Rico is no longer beside me. Sitting up, I look around the room, only to find he's not there either. There's a good deal of noise coming from downstairs, though, so I get dressed, then venture down.

At the bottom of the stairs, I'm greeted with questioning glares from barely-dressed women. There seems to be more, now, than earlier, and most of them are carrying drinks of varying colors, sipping at them as though they've got some sort of class. The way they're dripping off half of the men in the house, though, defeats that objective.

Still a little drunk on sleep, I make my way into the kitchen. Rico, Dieter and Sirus are around the breakfast bar. There're girls hanging off each of them, and, while Rico doesn't look the slight bit interested, my green-eyed bitch makes a bee-line for the red-haired slut all but nibbling on his ear lobe. It's the same dozy bint from before.

Well, stupidity like this deserves to be recognised.

I don't march up to her, instead, I glide, swaying my hips because I know – and she doesn't – that my honeyed façade will drop the moment I reach her. I want her to think I'm as fragile and twat-like as she is, before I knock her fucking teeth out. I want her to look at me, while in my head, I'm thinking, *that's right, bitch; I'm coming for you, and you've got no idea. You think you can stop me with a bitch slap, but I'm gonna ruin your face for all other men.*

She looks up at me, the sickly smile on her face dropping, somewhat. And then the false sense of security I'm luring her into pays off. Her smile switches to one more sugary. She's got a glean in her eye that my inner demon is loving right now.

Flicking her tongue out, she doesn't get close to swiping it across Rico's ear.

Lashing out my hand, I grab her around the throat, where her scream catches and dies. Her eyes bulge, before I draw my other fist back, punching her, square in the jaw. Her nose pops under the impact, stirring the butterflies in my stomach. "I warned out," I remind her, before I smash her face in for a second time.

Rico calls my name, asks me what I'm playing at, but really, I sense that he's getting off on my dominant display. His front is only for Dieter's benefit.

As the red-head runs off, crying, I turn to the three still sat at the table. Sirus is looking at me like a fat kid with an overflowing bag of sweets – it repulses me. Rico is trying so hard to hide his smile.

Dieter, however, looks detached, and that's what sets me on edge the most. I won't apologise, though; I'll wait until he says something, to see what he expects of me now that I've done what I have.

I tread carefully toward the table, sitting myself beside Rico, my eyes still pinned to Dieter, my face rigid. "How long until we're ready for this?" I swipe my hand over the plans for the job, purposely deferring away from the obvious.

"Are we ignoring the fact that you're just caved in the face of one of my girls?" Dieter's voice is dangerously low, but the twinkle in his eyes suggests he's not as mad as he's trying to make out.

"You mean, like she ignored the fact that I warned her to keep her grubby hands of *my* man?" I don't know what's possessing me to be so brave, but I can't help it. I believe that if I don't shy away from this man, that he will understand my worth; keep me around, get me involved in more and more of his business. It might be foolish, but it's a risk I'm willing to gamble on.

"A word." Dieter stands, while my stomach plummets.

Following him, he takes us into his office, then shuts the door. Turning to me, he throws out his hand, slapping my face with the back of it.

The sting lances through my jaw, but I resist the temptation to touch the throb as I stare at Dieter, trying to guess what might be coming next.

"While I admire your balls, Asha, there's a fine line between confidence and arrogance." He walks around to his desk, pulls out two glasses and a bottle of bourbon from one of the drawers, before he pours one for each of us. He hands me the tumbler. "You'd do well to make sure there's less of the latter, because you know full well, I do not suffer fools."

I'm torn between telling him to get fucked, or swallowing my pride and apologising. I need to stay in his good graces, so I accept the liquor, knock it back, then tell him, "I'm sorry. I didn't mean to step on any toes."

"Nor did you, but the next time you show me attitude like that, I'll start hacking off parts of your body. Is that understood?"

He's not lying; I know from experience that when Dieter says he will do something, he will do exactly that. "Understood." I nod, handing him back the empty glass.

Face still smarting, I take my leave when Dieter points toward the door. Rico is waiting for me in the foyer. His face scrunches up when he sees the state of mine; Dieter must have left quite the impression, as Rico's body tenses when he comes close, before he places a soft touch to my cheek.

"I got off lightly," I tell him, hoping that it will be enough to appease him. Last thing anyone needs is Rico going off, thinking he can take on Dieter over a measly slap. "I shouldn't be so cocky."

A smile hitches at the corners of his mouth, somewhat beautifying the scowl. "I love your cockiness." He kisses my forehead, then takes my hand, pulling me through to the vast expanse of Dieter's lounge.

Dieter loves to flash his cash, and his home is decked out in original Edwardian furniture and art. Floor to ceiling bay windows look out onto a huge garden and vineyard in impeccable condition. Two Dobermans chase one another around the stunning array of greens, reds, oranges and purples, and scores of bikini-clad, buxom women still squeal delighted noises from around one of the other pools.

It's like walking onto a fucking movie set; it's so cliché it's almost sickening.

Some guys are sat around a large, glass table near the back of the room. It's here that Rico takes me, by the hand. "Come on," he soothes, "let's get you a little more relaxed."

I hadn't realised that I needed to relax, but as he says it, I feel the muscles in my shoulders tense up. Maybe I'm a little more vexed at Dieter's assault on me than I want to believe.

When we get closer to the table, I see exactly what Rico means by *relax*. The guys are doing lines of coke while they play cards.

I'm not sure I wanna do this. I've been around drugs for years, but that doesn't mean that I've taken any of that shit up my nose. "I'm good." I go for reassuring, nonchalant, but I don't know if it's believable.

Rico looks at me. “Are you kidding me? Your body’s rigid as fuck; I’ve never seen you like this before.”

Christ, he’s really going to make me do this, like it’s the most natural thing in the world. I suppose, for these guys, it is; and now they’re expecting that it should be a walk in the park for me, too – that I’m used to this.

I’m torn. There’s a war raging inside my head right now. On one hand, I don’t want to get even remotely close to losing my senses, risk saying something I might regret, thinking that I’m invincible when I’m not. On the other hand, if I don’t do this, they’re going to grow suspicious of me.

Maybe a small amount won’t have quite the effect I’m dreading. “We’ve got a job to do in a few hours; is this wise?” I’ve gotta try one last ditch attempt at getting out of this. “This is my first job, guys, I can’t afford to fuck this up if I’m off my tits, or dying to drop where I stand when that shit wears off.”

Chuckling, Rico measures me out a small line. He thinks I'm joking. Either that, or he doesn't give a shit. He's determined to see me relaxed.

Maybe it won't be as bad as I'm thinking. I've known individuals to have mixed reactions when snorting coke. Some have wanted more, others have wondered what all the fuss was about. With luck on my side, and such a small amount, I'll fall into the second category.

Whatever happens, though, I'm going to have to do this.

Handing me a rolled-up note, Rico puts his hand on my shoulder. "I got something to numb the effects of the come down; you'll be fine, babe. You just need to loosen up a little, take the edge off today."

I try so hard to stop my body from shaking, gently moving away from Rico's touch as I nod. Sitting at the table, I take a deep breath, place the bank note to my nose, use a finger to close off the other nostril, then bend down to the table.

Hair falls over my face, almost making me scream out victorious. I use the moment of distraction to flick away a good portion of the powder, as I inhale the remaining small amount up my nose.

Leaning back, I close my eyes, feeling the numbness in my nose, throat and mouth. The pain of it is almost pleasurable. I don't much care whether taking less makes a difference, the feeling of such celestial euphoria makes me feel like I'm floating on clouds, away from the suffering, the pain, the madness. I can feel my heart beating faster, in light flurries against my chest as a burst of energy detonates in my limbs.

I can hear the dogs in the garden, sniffing at the grass and I want to go and join them. I want to roll around with them, feel the cold, sleek shards of each green blade sweep across my naked flesh.

The pain in my cheek isn't there anymore; it's drifted away with all my other cares.

Opening my eyes, Rico stands over me, a large grin on his handsome face. He's so beautiful, it makes my heart ache. Maybe he'd want to come and roll around outside with me. We could be naked together, feel nature embrace us as one.

I stand, still feeling like I'm floating with each step I take. Rico's hand is in mine, and we're heading toward the back garden.

The air-headed bimbos aren't bothering me right now; the noise they're making dissipates into the background. I'm not even concerned with the dogs, as they sniff around my feet. I just want to lie on the grass with Rico.

For near on ten minutes, we lie still, staring at the stars in the clear, night sky. Weariness then washes over me, my body sags, feeling heavier than usual. I want that feeling of heavenly paradise back, but my senses are returning to me, telling me that that would not be a good idea.

With sweaty palms, I push myself up, feeling a little agitated and short of breath.

"You OK?" Rico's voice disturbs my calm, making me almost uneasy.

I gotta keep my shit together, though. "I'm fine." It feels like there's a nest of ants running under my skin, but I resist the urge to scratch and maul myself to get rid of them.

"Here." Rico hands me a small white pill.

I'm taken aback that he wants me to take *more* drugs. Can my body handle this? "What is it?" I'm wary; it could be anything – it could even finish me off.

"Benzodiazepine. It'll take the edge off the negatives you'll be experiencing." Rico takes one himself, then smiles at me, nodding.

Pissed that I'm having yet more drugs, I throw the pill to the back of my throat and swallow it, hoping it doesn't take long to have an effect. I'm certain the side effects of sniffing that shit are not worth the end result, and I'm glad I didn't take any more than what I did.

*

It's well after midnight, and, free of my abnormal state – aside from feelings associated with being a complete moron – we're seated on plush sofas in Dieter's lounge, being offered cognac by his butler, and sandwiches from his maid. I have a hard time reeling in my anger because I know how he manages to afford all this. It's the reason I'm here – for the most part.

"Asha, let me welcome you to the crew you'll be working with." Dieter's Cuban brogue brings me crashing back to reality. He nods toward Rico and Sirus. "You know these two, already." Holding his palm out to a beefy black guy with a bald head and scary as fuck, dark eyes, he tells me, "This is Leo. You can probably gather he's the muscle, but he will supply you with whatever you need."

I salute Leo with a blasé flick of my wrist before Dieter draws my attention to two scrawny, long-haired blonde blokes who look very much alike.

"Harris and Frankie; they're our…sales team. And the brains behind the operation is Lucas." He nods at a tanned, slim but muscled guy in glasses, sat behind a computer. He's hot in a sexy, geeky kinda way. I'd expect to see him on the cover of some model magazine for designer eyewear.

Pulling my attention back to him, Dieter claps his hands together. "Let's get down to business, shall we?"

Lucas pipes up from behind his screen, "Arrival is due in oh three hundred hours, we got two guys on the beach already, and Leo will soon be heading out to the warehouse to secure our transport." He looks at Leo, then at Rico and me. "You guys will be two of the guns; make sure you're trained on the driver coming in, take him out first opportunity, somewhere near this pass." He points to a spot on the map, some ways from the beach, so as to avoid any noise alerting anyone else. "We know there's gonna be guys on the beach already, so once he's out of the picture, head down and be where you need to be."

Fabulous, more death. Not that these assholes don't deserve it. However, for the time being, it's mindless – the drugs are still gonna end up on the street, one way or another. Some poor kid is still gonna OD on this shit, more than likely. On the other hand, I need some of this shit for Bruno, so I need to be on top form tonight, or things could go very badly, very quickly.

Lucas continues, "Benny and Jase will grab the gear. After that, haul ass to the car 'cuz we won't be waiting around too long. The beach is manned. We'll have ten minutes, tops."

"Asha," Dieter says, "Rico will fill you in on what I expect. Everyone, back here in an hour to kit up and move out."

*

The hotel room swirls around me as I sit on the edge of the bed, rubbing my hands up and down my freshly-washed face, tapping out a nervous beat on the floor with my feet.

You can do this; you're ready for it. Who gives a shit what happens to the rest of these idiots tonight, they're scum anyway – even the ones you're gonna waste; they'd be getting their comeuppance sooner or later. You're just cutting out the middle man. Just bide your time, grab the gear, get out and let what happens, happen.

Reaching down toward the floor, I pick up my glass of whiskey, knocking it back in one, scrunching my eyes together as the burn heats my throat. My pep talk doesn't make me feel much better, but it's gotta be done. I'm used to situations more organised and planned out, and, to a degree, this is, but I have my own game plan – one I need to keep secret from absolutely everyone – and if I don't execute it perfectly, then I'll be dead before dawn.

My phone vibrates inside my bag and I grab for it, swiping the screen to retrieve my text message:

UPDATE?

I fire off a quick response about the meeting time and location, as well as how many men we can expect on both sides, but I warn them that there's gonna be a lot of firepower, they need to stay back; let me do what needs to be done while they stay out of sight. This is only small fry; it isn't what we're looking for. I just hope everyone understands that, and takes my advice. Unbeknown to them, my own safety and selfish needs are also at stake.

As my message sends, a beep from my laptop draws my attention. Rico is parking up outside the hotel.

When my phone vibrates in my hand, I let out a gasp, looking at the screen to see Warren's name flashing. "Shit." I hit the button to connect the call, preying with everything in me that Rico doesn't walk in before I'm finished.

Chapter 6

"I need more information than this." Warren isn't happy; I can tell by the low tolerance in his tone. "I'm happy to go in on this job and wipe them out."

"No, you can't." I so badly need for him to listen to me, fast; I need more time, but I can't tell him that without raising suspicion. "It's small fry, we've been waiting for bigger shipments, this will be a waste of our resources." My voice is shaking, hurried, but I don't have time to care about that right now.

Letting out a heavy breath, taking all the goddamn time in the world to answer, Warren tells me, "That's not for you to decide. Why do you think it's not gonna pay off?"

I need to think quicker than ever before. Rico is already inside the hotel, it won't be long before he reaches my door – and I gave him a key earlier. "Dieter doesn't have even half of his man-power on this, which tells me it's a small job in comparison to what could be coming." My palms are starting to sweat. Warren cannot use this job as the be all and end of all of what he's trying to do - I need this so that I can get the drugs for Bruno and exchange them for vital information. "Trust me," I continue, hoping that he will listen to far-fetched reason. "I've been working for these guys for months now, following their movements for years. This is not the job we want." I emphasise my final point slowly. "It's your call, Tony, but, believe me, it'll be a complete waste of time, money and effort. If there's ever a time to trust me, trust me now." I realise the irony of my statement, but I can't let Warren mess this up for me.

He's taking too long to decide; my heart is beating a panicked path up my chest and into my throat. Rico will be here any minute.

"Tony," I plead once more, before my hotel room door bursts open and Rico strolls in, two beers and two brown bags with food in hand.

“What’s up, baby? Who you calling?”

I panic. My heart slams against my chest, my palms sweaty. "I'm not calling anyone," I rush, while trying not to. "My battery died." Turning the phone away from Rico, I hold down the power button, watching the screen fade as he walks over and dumps our dinner on the table.

He takes the phone outta my hand before throwing it down on the bed behind me. "You hungry? I got Cheeseburgers." He grabs hold of my shoulders, leaning in to kiss my forehead.

"Starving." My voice quivers, my hands still trembling as I hide them from his line of sight.

"You OK, darl', you're a bit shaky?"

I can do nothing but nod, afraid my voice will be betray me further.

Rico stands in front of me, reaffirming his grip on my shoulders with a squeeze. "You're bound to be nervous, but you got this. Look what you did with Marco."

Thank fuck; he thinks I'm edgy about the job. I can work with that. "I know, babe, but this is different. There're more people involved; more lives to look out for, other than my own. I don't wanna fuck up, and I certainly don't wanna get anyone killed because I can't focus." Not a complete lie, but it certainly isn't because I have any regard for the lives of the scum I'll be joining; they can all be dragged to hell by their still beating hearts, for all I care.

"You'll do great. I'll be there right along with you; I'll talk you through it."

"You do have a way with words," I purr, stroking my finger down his tight chest and stomach. "Maybe I just need to…unwind." There's something about the notion of getting my hands dirty that rubs me up the right way. It's morbid, I know, but part of me connects with violence on some level. Maybe because I know, deep down, it's justified. I'm doing people a favor, ridding the streets of these guys. Or so I tell myself.

He grabs my waist, then turns me, forcing me backwards until I'm sitting on the table. "Well, why didn't you say?" he growls, brushing the beers and food to the floor. "We'll get more." He winks when I look at the mess and smirk.

Wrapping my legs around him, I pull him close, taking his face in my hands, kissing his soft lips, gliding my tongue over his when he dips it into my mouth. My lust is returned when he forces me further back, pushing me with the strength of his embrace.

Ripping open my blouse, he squeezes my breasts together, leaning down to bite my nipple over the thin material of my red bra. His heated breath stiffens the receptive bud making me groan under the erotic assault, before he moves his attention to the other.

Reaching between us, I massage his cock. It's already full and hard as stone, throbbing in my hand. He hisses through his teeth, pressing his lips to mine, his tongue darting inside my mouth, desperate, exploring.

I squeal when he hauls me up and walks me to the bathroom, littering kisses down my neck and chest.

"Strip for me," he commands, putting me down.

With seductive slowness, I peel off my blouse, the tips of my fingers brushing the hardness of my nipples. I close my eyes, take in a deep breath as charged bolts of pleasure burn through my chest. The garment slides down my arms, landing on the floor in a heap around my feet. Opening my eyes, I stare at Rico as I thumb the waistband of my jeans. I pop open the buttons one by one, then slip them down my legs with provocative elegance. Rising, I stand before him in my underwear, biting my bottom lip, waiting for him to make a move.

"You're so fuckin' hot, Asha." He flips the shower on, then takes off his clothes, standing before me in all of his buff, naked glory.

The guy is a sight to behold. He's tall, tanned and rippled with muscle. His dick is large, thick and beautiful, and it throbs between his robust thighs as he stares at me.

I remove my bra and panties, sliding a hand between my legs, feeling my heated excitement. A quivering breath escapes his lips when I dip a finger into my drenched core and draw it to my lips.

He's on me in an instant, pinning me against the wall, forcing his lips on mine. He invades my mouth with his thrusting tongue while he cups my sodden sex in the palm of his large hand. I gasp, melting into him when he slips two fingers inside, curling them upward, roughly grazing them against my insides with deliberate teasing.

"You're so ready for me," he utters in my ear, giving me goose bumps along my tickled skin.

Drawing out of me, he grabs my hand and leads me toward the steaming shower, allowing me entry into the hot spray of the water first.

Once in, he traps me between his hands – pressed against the glass – and lowers his wet lips to mine. His mouth is hot, his tongue gliding a slippery path across mine when he thrusts it into me. Moaning against him, I slide my hands up his sleek, brawny arms, gripping his biceps while he leans further in.

"I'm gonna help you relax, babe. Tonight, is all about you."

Two fingers penetrate my slick opening, making me gasp at the erogenous invasion. My back is pressed firmly against the cold glass behind me, sending a mixture of sensations through my sensitised skin.

He strokes my walls with pressured movements, thumbing my clit at the same time. My mouth parts, releasing a strangled moan while I arch my hips into his touch. Deeper he delves and harder he strums, whispering wanton promises in my ear, as my body begins to lighten, overcome with a feeling of freedom.

Every touch, every thought, every sound detaches itself from my being as I start to feel as though I am floating; my body no longer my own.

Rico grips my waist, thrusting in and out of my clenching pussy, littering my neck and chest with fevered kisses, immersing me in a blistering heat that puckers my skin, bringing me back to reality, crashing through as every sensation returns tenfold.

I palm the glass behind me, groaning, mouthing his name before I clamp down on his fingers and come apart around him.

I throw my arms around his neck, my body pressed against his, struggling to stay upright, yet, still he drives in, coaxing out every drop of my release while I shudder against him.

With slow, teasing, movements, he draws out.

My legs buckle, my stomach still clenching with the remnants of my climax, my breathing heavy, shaking.

Rico is there to hold me steady, using the strength of his burly build to hold me, tight against him.

Every drop from the shower makes me shudder, my bare, flushed skin tender to even the slightest of touches.

Even Rico's whispered words make me shiver, my body vulnerable and tender. "Feel better, sweetheart?"

I can only nod with a smile.

*

After Rico's carnal invasion of me in the shower, my body begged for respite. But there would be no time for that until after the job.

Sitting in Rico's car, my body feels heavy, almost lethargic, yet hugely gratified. I want to lean my head back, close my eyes, allow myself to drift off listening to the steady, rhythmic purr of the engine.

Only, I can't. I need to wake up if I'm to focus on this job. It's one thing to let down my guard, get those around me killed; but it'll be a cold, hard kick in the bollocks if I end up taking a bullet myself. Then all of this would have been for nothing.

Rico has his game face on.

As I stare at him from the corner of my eye, I note the rigid flex in his jaw, his eyes fixed to the road ahead. His beautiful features are illuminated by the bright blues and whites of the dashboard lights, yet the shadows of the night outside give him a more sinister guise.

His lips hitch up into a smirk – he knows I'm looking at him, gawking like a horny teenager at the first sight of her naked boyfriend's body.

"Like what you see?"

I even find his arrogance charming, and I can't help but return his smile, nodding, knowing that he can see me do it.

Caught up in the moment, I place my hand on his knee, slowly sliding it further up his thigh until I'm cupping the generous bulge in his pants. Pulling my bottom lip between my teeth, I reach for his zipper, undoing it, desperate to get at the erogenous treasure inside.

Rico growls, adjusting himself in his seat to allow me better access.

Again, he's not wearing any underwear, and my body breaks out in tingles of anticipation when I feel the red-hot heat of his already hardened cock against my probing fingers.

When I lean down and take the tip of him between my lips, his body bucks, jolting back into the chair. He hisses between his teeth, and I hear the scrunch of the leather steering wheel as his grip around it tightens.

Our positioning only allows me to tease him, so I use my tongue to stroke the head of length, my teeth, too, to graze his tender flesh.

"Shit, Asha!" Rico grabs hold of my hair, pulling me from him in time for me to see the body of an animal – a dog, perhaps, smash into the windscreen before going over the top of us.

Rico has already reacted, though. He turns the steering wheel first one way, then the other, trying to even out the car as we skid across the road. The windscreen is obliterated; I can feel the cool air whooshing inside the car, hear it whistling from outside.

Something wet and warm trickles down my forehead.

I don't have time to contemplate it, as the car careens off the road, down a grassy and embankment before smashing, head on, into a tree.

My head snaps to the side, cracking off the window. Acute pains shoot down my spine, over and over. It intensifies the harder I breathe in and out. My vision fades, reappears, then fades again, blurring together colors and shapes like a Monet painting, intermittently dotted with shooting stars firing in a mixture of all directions.

Trying to turn my head in Rico's direction, I cry out as fresh agony cripples me.

Rico is slumped forward, blood oozing from a gash in his head. His eyes are closed, but I can see the steady rise and fall of his chest.

Funnily enough, as I sit here, my aching body riddled with burning pain, my last thought – before I succumb to the welcomed, obsidian mass clouding my brain, is that the doctors are going to know *exactly* what we were doing before we ran ourselves off the road.

Chapter 7

The moment I open my eyes, the battering my body took comes back with a vengeance. Every inch of me hurts beyond comparison, like I've been stomped on by an army of men, then thrown to wolves so that they could tear at my flesh, finishing me off, devouring me whole.

I want to cry out, but I don't know where I am. The lights in the room with me are blinding, and it's taking me a great deal of blinking past their brilliance to even begin to contemplate my whereabouts.

I can hear voices, some distance away, perhaps in another room. There's a slight echo to them, as though their surroundings are vast, or sparsely decorated, not something you would expect to find in someone's home. A low beeping sound interrupts my thoughts with its recurring tone.

Trying to piece together the events of the evening, my brain jumps into action, gauging that I am likely in a hospital. The only beeping I can hear is the one close to me, so I surmise that I am alone in my room, as opposed to being on a ward with others. The voices I can hear are most likely the nurses stationed outside.

I allow myself to groan against the beating in my bones.

“She’s awake.” The voice is female, soft-spoken and aged, with an accent not too common around these parts.

A face appears above me, though distorted by my still-unfocused vision. I can tell her skin is dark; it’s a stark contract against the silver of her short hair.

The more my sight returns, the more I can make out of the mature, smiling face above me. The Jamaican woman is easily in her sixties, if not older. Her mocha-tinted eyes are lined with wrinkles, but there’s a glowing kindness behind them that puts me at ease.

“Can you hear me, sweetheart?” She places a warm hand on my forehead, then against my wrist before she averts her attention to other areas of my beaten body. Her touch is so tender, but sends signals of pain and torment to my brain, making every trace burn with prickled heat.

“How long… .” They’re the only words I can manage, but she understands.

With a smile, she tells me, “A few hours. It’s not as bad as it likely feels at the moment.” With that, she tinkers with a drip beside my bed, making my pain easier to handle, as it subsides somewhat.

God bless painkillers.

Clearing my throat, I try another question. “The man… I was with.” I can’t manage anything more than that.

“He’s OK.” Her smile isn’t as strong, making my stomach turn. “He’s still unconscious at the moment, but he’s stable.” Turning, she reaches for a jug of water, pouring me a small measure. “You both took quite a battering when you hit the tree, but you’ll live.” Her smiling face reappears as she tries to feed me small sips.

I’m grateful; my mouth feels like an animal took a shit in it. “What’s the damage?”

“You have a concussion, small laceration on your head; nothing too severe. You’ll have a headache for a couple of days though. On the bright side,” she notes, placing my cup down, “there’s no broken bones, so you should be out in the next day or two. The doctor just wants to monitor you for a while.”

Panic sets in – along with a swift, heavy reminder as to why we were on the road in the first place. The job! I can’t have missed this opportunity; too much is riding on it. “What time is it?” I try to sit up, wincing as my sore body protests.

“It’s almost four-thirty, my dear.”

Fuck! Shitting, bastard fuck sticks, we've missed it. Oh god, Dieter is going to be pissed. I doubt he's expressing any concerns over our no-show – or, at least, certainly not mine. How the hell are we going to explain this to him? I mean, one can't help getting involved in a road accident, I suppose, but is he going to be that empathetic when this could have cost him millions in drugs?

And what about Bruno and my timeframe? That's one gang leader who *will not* accept any excuse short of death, and, even then, he'd still dig you up to piss on your rotting carcass for the inconvenience you've caused him.

Without this morning's job, there's no way I'm going to have what he's asked of me in time.

I need to get out of here, rethink my strategy. Perhaps the job still went ahead, perhaps there's still bodies and drugs littered on the beach? It's a long shot, a one-in-a-million chance that luck is going to be on my side enough to grant me this small mercy, but it's all I've got to cling on to.

When the nurse leaves, I battle against the pain to pull out whatever's attached to me. I'm in hospital attire, but my bloody clothes are folded and bagged on a chair in the room.

Dressing quickly, still trying to ignore the aches and throbs, I head for the door, checking up and down the corridors for signs of life.

There's nurses and orderlies milling around, but if I'm relaxed about it, I can meander right by them without drawing much attention to myself. *Just act cool; as though nothing is amiss, and you're not even meant to be here.* Despite the cuts and bruises I must be covered in.

I've no choice, so, edging out of the room, I try my luck, holding my head up, moving out of the room and down the corridor as though I belong here – even if my heart is pounding against my chest like the contradicting bitch that she is, desperate to give me away.

Winding my way around corridor after corridor, following the exit signs, my heart skips a beat when I see the doors leading outside. There's isn't too much in the way of security around, and they'd have no real reason to stop me, anyway. I take a deep breath, heading straight for them.

The air is crisp, hitting me with a chilled blast when the automatic doors slide open. Maybe it's because my body is over-sensitive from the wreckage; I don't know, all I know is that it hurts. But I ignore it, instead flagging down a cab to take me to the beach. I know it's risky, but I'm desperate. I'll have the driver drop me a safe distance away, just in case.

I give him the directions before he sets off. Each bump in the road throws fresh torment around my insides. My head throbs in more places than I care to count, and I make a mental note to grab some pain relief at the first opportunity.

I don't know whether it's because of the agony I'm in, or the inner turmoil I'm drowning in from the thought of Bruno and his missing drugs, but the journey to the beach seems to take a hell of a lot longer than it should. Maybe it's a mixture, coupled with the uncertainty of what I'm going to find when I get there, plus the aftermath of Dieter's ire at us being missing from one of his heists.

Shit! *Rico.* I forgot to check on him before I left. I'm so consumed with the thought of getting what I need, that I've completely forgotten about him still lying in a hospital bed. Fuck. I can't exactly go back to Dieter without at least some knowledge of his condition. The mob boss will ask questions, and if I can't answer him, my brain matter will make for an additional coat of paint on his walls. He'll think this is my fault, that somehow, I've betrayed him.

Things are just getting shittier and shittier.

I can only take one thing at a time, though. First off, I need to see what state this heist has been left in.

When the cab driver comes to a stop, my heart is my mouth, a queasy feeling circling in my stomach. I throw him some cash, tell him to keep the change, then get out. The walk to the beach isn't too far, but already I can see flashing blue lights over the hills leading toward it. The sickness in my belly only intensifies.

Keeping a safe distance, I peer over toward the beach. There are a few cop cars lining the sand, some of the occupants pacing the beach, as a crime scene team analyses what looks to be the aftermath of a shoot-out.

"Shit." I run a hand through my knotted hair, flinching when I catch the cut on my head. I hope to God Dieter didn't show when me and Rico didn't turn up at his house. Saying that, though, whether he did or didn't, there's no way he's going to believe that I had nothing to do with this.

My dilemma, now, is do I turn up and plead my case, blood, bruises and all as proof or our accident, or do I try and score more dope for Bruno before my window of opportunity closes, and I lose everything I've worked for, for the past two years?

*

As far as Dieter is concerned, I'm still AWOL. I could still be lying in the hospital next to Rico, for all he knows. Until he discovers what's happened, my whereabouts is pretty safe… ish. I don't think anyone paid much attention to me when I went back to the hotel to change.

At least, that's what I'm trying to convince myself of as I walk down the alley toward Bruno's bar.

This isn't going to go well, not in the slightest. He got pissed the last time I showed up, unannounced. Now, I'm going to be showing up unannounced, *and* minus the ten bags of premium coke he's expecting from me. I'm still a few days away from the deadline, so, maybe he will go easy on me, perhaps extend once he sees the state of me. I'll play on it; milk it as much as I can.

I know that's bullshit, though, even as I think about it. I almost laugh at the pomposity of such a notion, but my situation is too dire to force a smile.

It's still early, so there aren't many people in the bar as I open the door. The bartender gives me the same nonchalant look he always does, and I receive a few quick glances off the patrons, but they're too busy drinking and talking their lives away to pay me much consideration.

I don't even ask the barman if Bruno is upstairs, I just head on over and up. I hear him tutting behind me, calling me rude. *Shit happens, pal.*

Every step I take, I wonder how I'm going to handle this. I can't really knock, he'll blow a hole in me through the door the moment I tell him it's me. He'll likely do the same as soon as I barge in, but at least I'll have the element of surprise in my favor.

Drawing my gun from the waistband of my jeans, I ready it in front of me, my free hand hovering over the door handle. I swear, my breathing must be easily audible through the wood of the door, but it's difficult to say for sure over the pounding of my heart in my brain.

With a deep breath, I throw the door open, making a quick observation of the room.

Three men, including Bruno, all around one table. Lucky for me.

They all snap their heads to my attention, drawing weapons. As they point theirs at me, I level mine at Bruno's head.

"Don't even think about it." Thankfully, my voice doesn't crack. "I need a word with you." I nod in Bruno's direction, looking at him square in the eyes, yet staying vigilant of the other two.

Bruno turns in his chair, so that he is facing me more fully, a cigarette hanging between his lips. "And you thought this was the way to get it?" Smoke billows from his mouth. "You look like shit." Standing, he takes the cigarette from his mouth, throwing it to the floor before grinding it out with his foot. Not once does he take his eyes off me.

"Perks of ramming a car into a tree. I need more time." I can't beat around the bush, that's not a luxury I have. "Last night was the night I was going to get what you wanted, only, fate intervened."

"Yeah, she's a bitch." He nods to something behind me. "But the answer's no."

Hands grab me from behind, one gliding down my arm to take the gun from me. This isn't going to end well.

I throw my head back, grinning when I hear a crack, but wincing at the throb in my own body.

The man behind me stumbles, holding his nose as blood seeps between his fingers. The gun's skidded across the floor, though, so it's out of my immediate reach.

Drawing back my open palm, I used my free hand to move the guy's from his face, then I slam my palm into the base of his nose. For precious seconds, he glares at me with wide eyes, before they roll back into his head. He drops to the floor, lifeless.

I turn back to Bruno, who looks at me in wonderment, but has still found time to retrain his gun on me. I am defenceless.

His nostrils flare, jaw twitching as he stomps toward me. He backhands me with the butt of his gun and I crumble to the floor, clutching my bleeding head.

"You're lucky I'm feeling generous, and that Eddie was an asshole." Bruno crouches to my level, getting in my face. "Rather than kill you here, I'm just going to cut your timescale down. You've got one day, or I will shoot you in the face." He pulls a piece of paper from his pocket, wafting it in my face. "I have what you want, so you had better get what I want, or this, and you, go up in flames."

One day? I'll never get what he needs in one day, not unless Dieter has something else lined up for tonight, and providing *he* doesn't want to kill me on sight, either. Is it a chance I can take? I don't see that I have much in the way of a choice; I'm outnumbered and outgunned at the moment. If I say no, he'll slaughter me right now.

"Fine." We both know it's impossible. I think that Bruno is just enjoying prolonging my torment, and is actually looking forward to the moment he can put a bullet between my eyes. Why the charade, though, I don't know. It does, however, give *me* time to also plan how the hell I'm going to get away with this, *and* get the information I need.

Chapter 8

The sunlight on the streets hurts my head. I'm getting funny stares from people looking at the state of my face; not one of them bothers to ask me if I'm OK, though. Clearly, I'm fine because I'm walking unaided, so, I guess they must think I don't need any help.

I don't, but it would just be common courtesy to at least ask. People suck.

Back in my hotel room, I clean up, yet again, changing into clothes a little fresher after a shower. I need to go and see how Rico is doing; if I'm going to get back into Dieter's good graces, it might help to have him by my side.

I'm also preying that he's got another job lined up, or some drugs lying around the house that I can swipe. Though, how I'd get out of his house alive with ten bags stashed in my jeans is beyond me, but I'm getting desperate, and time is quickly running out.

The journey back to the hospital is in silence; the only time either one of us speaks is when I thank the driver and hand him some cash.

I wonder if any of the nurses might recognise me when I go back in, maybe chastise me for upping and leaving without a word. As I walk through the doors, I need not have worried; it seems a lot quieter than it did in the early hours of the morning.

Walking toward the reception desk, I ask the middle-aged lady where I might find Rico, with a quick explanation of how he ended up in here. She looks at me with a little suspicion as her eyes squint, likely at the cuts and bruises marring my face, but she doesn't say anything, only tells me what floor Rico is on.

Heading for the elevator, I'm a little worried at the state I'm going to find him in. The nurse said he's stable, but unconscious. What if his state of unconsciousness lasts a long time? What if he doesn't remember me? What if he takes one look at me, realises he could do better, and tells me to fuck off? I realise I'm rambling inside my own head, right now, but there's sod all else to do as the lift ascends to the floor I need.

When the doors open, I release a deep breath I didn't realise I'd been holding. Wow, elevators are claustrophobic when you've got nothing but your idiotic thoughts for company.

I find the corridor I want, then head toward the room I now know Rico is in.

He's hooked up to a similar machine that I was, earlier this morning. His face is a little ashen, but he's breathing. His eyes are closed, though. I don't know if that's a good thing, or a bad thing, yet.

I slide myself into the chair next to his bed, slipping my hand into his clammy one.

He stirs, murmuring something unintelligible, before his eyes flicker open. His head turns to my direction, but even the slow movement looks painful for him. He's not in a neck brace, though, so, surely, it can't be that bad.

"Asha?" His voice is dry, throaty, much like mine was when I first came around.

Relieved that he is awake, I reach toward the beside unit for the jug, then pour him a small glass of water, hold it to his lips, while I help him take small sips to wet his throat enough to talk without wanting to cough up a lung.

"I'm here, babe," I reassure him, "I'm not going anywhere." At least, not yet.

It takes some time for Rico to regain a coherent speech, enough for him to be able to string together a legible sentence. He asks me what happened.

I'm a little embarrassed when I remind him, but he smirks at the recollection, which puts me a little at ease that he's still able to find the funny side to this mess.

"We missed the job." No sense in beating around the bush; he'd ask eventually, and we need to conjure up some way of appealing to Dieter's good side, when we return to his villa to explain our no show.

His lack of a response, but the expectant look in his face when he nods once, tells me he kinda figured out that much by himself. After all, it's daylight outside; the sun is shining brightly through his open window. Considering it was dark when we should have been there, it doesn't take a genius to work it all out.

"What do you think Dieter's going to say?" My heart misses a beat when I ask the question, but, with what I do know about his lack of patience, I don't actually know if our predicament – of which could have technically been avoided, but we won't tell him that – will make the slightest bit of difference when we tell him what happened.

Rico shrugs his shoulders. "It's not like we crashed on purpose."

True. "I don't think we need to tell him how it happened, though. Let's just blame it on the animal running across the road and leave out all the other stuff." I laugh, a nervous sound.

"Agreed."

I tell him that I went to check it out, only to find the place overrun with investigators and police. I didn't see any of our men, nor Wick's, so there's no comfort or guarantee that we've come off on top here, or any evidence to suggest that Dieter put it off due to be short-handed. If it's the latter, he's not going to be happy – that shipment was worth a lot of money and contacts to him. We are going to need to do some serious sucking up.

Rico's able to come home as the afternoon draws in, which is a relief, since I'm getting agitated that I've been sat with him for a good portion of the day, and I'm no closer to finding a solution to my Bruno problem. I want to say something to Rico, but I know that would be the dumbest idea I've ever had. How would I even begin to explain why I know him, why I need to supply him with drugs? No, it's totally stupid … or is it? Maybe I can work this to my advantage. I'll need to have a good think about how I can manipulate this situation to come out in my favor.

"Rico, I need your help." After what's happened to us, I think it's about time I placed a little bit of trust in the man I … love? "I'm in trouble."

*

During the journey back to Dieters, my nerves are shot to shit. I don't know whether that's because I'm anxious over what he will say, or whether I'm scared we'll end up in another accident en route. Either way, I don't even think about touching Rico until we're safely out of the moving, speeding vehicle.

I've told Rico what I can; what I feel comfortable with. It's not the entire truth, but it's enough to, hopefully, sort out the predicament with Bruno. I don't want Dieter knowing just yet, though; there'll be a time and a place for that, but I am hoping it's going to be sooner rather soon.

When Dieter's villa comes into view, I want to be sick. My face drains of all warmth, body shaking, palms sweaty. *For God's sake, why did I get involved in all of this.* Only, I know why, and I wouldn't do things any differently.

It's a strain to hold myself upright when I get out of the car. Using the roof to steady myself, I close the door with my other hand, then stare at Rico, begging him not to make me go in there.

"It'll be fine, Asha, I promise." He comes around my side of the vehicle, takes hold of my hand, giving it a gentle squeeze, then leads me toward the doors of Dieter's home.

Letting himself in, he calls out for the mob boss.

A few of his cronies walk into the lobby, Sirus is one of them. I certainly haven't missed his face, especially as the disgusting leer he gives me reminds my crawling skin what a lecherous dog he is.

"Nice of you to drop in," he smirks at the both of us, "been busy?"

"Go fuck yourself, where's Dieter?" Rico doesn't let go of my hand, instead, he lightly pulls me toward the kitchen, where I can now see cigar smoke being dispelled from.

Dieter is around the table with a couple of his men. When I see them all, glaring daggers at us, I have to swallow past the hot bile trying to make a fast, messy exit from my stomach.

Dieter isn't looking at us, however, when he asks, "Where have you been?"

"Hospital." It just blurts out, I can't stop myself, despite the fear and panic arguing among themselves for dominance, I just can't stop the word from tumbling out, since he hasn't the decency to look at us while he's talking to us. I find it rude, and, apparently, rudeness trumps all other traits and emotions today.

Nevertheless, it does afford us a double-take from him. "Take a seat." He gestures with a wave of his hand for his men to shift, so that we can be seated at the table. "What happened?" His fixed, flat tone doesn't give much away with regards to how he's feeling about our absence, and subsequent re-arrival.

I open my mouth to say more, but Rico jumps in before I can put my foot in it further.

"Animal on the road, we crashed into a tree, woke up in hospital this morning."

He's trying not to show fear, but I can feel the mild shaking through Rico's hand, which I still have clasped under the table.

"It wasn't our fault, D," he continues, lying through his teeth, "we were on our way when it happened."

For long moments, Dieter is quiet, staring at us, making me feel uneasy, and I feel, for sure, he's going to plant one between our eyes.

"Alright," he finally says, "I already had my guys check it out; they found your car. As a result, we didn't go through with the job."

Probably just as well, given the amount of uniforms on the beach this morning. It's reminding me to have a word with Warren about it, when I get the chance to. If I find he went against my advice, I'll go mad at him – he could've fucked everything up, and for what? A few criminals and some drugs. It would have hardly been worth the effort.

"Job's tonight."

I can barely believe my ears, or my luck. This could work out beautifully. I look at Rico, trying to suppress my knowing smile. He remains impassive, while I work out in my head, how I can use this massive snippet of information to my increasing advantage.

"Same set up as before," Dieter tells us, handing out maps and other bits of paper. "Different stretch of beach, different rival, same operation. And you two," he barks, pointing at us, "will stay here until it goes down. We don't want any more *accidents* now, do we?" Oh, he's definitely pissed – he can't say fuck all, because it wasn't our fault, as far as he knows, but he is most certainly pissed at having missed the job. Perhaps if he knew the outcome, he wouldn't feel so bad, but there's no way I'm telling him what I saw.

The only issue I have now, is, how the hell do I speak to Warren before the job goes down? Or, is it best that I don't, to save him from screwing it up all over again for me?

*

I hate Dieter; I hate everything he stands for. But, at this moment in time, my groaning, aching body is loving the soothing heat of the hot water I'm sat in, in a bath tub that could easily fit four people.

Steam rises from my pink skin, the scent of lavender and ylang ylang tickles my sense of smell with beautiful, tranquil aromas. It's a familiar smell, one I could give in to right now, fall asleep in such peaceful bliss as the deliciously warm water laps at my body like a thousand soft, stroking hands.

It's what I need. If I'm going to be camped out on the beach for who knows how many hours, then my body needs to be a little less tense than it is.

A knock at the unlocked door disturbs me somewhat, enough for me to hum an incoherent, "Who is it?" from between my lips.

Eyes closed, I hear the door click open, close, and the latch bolt into place. I open one eye, tilting my head toward the source of my intrusion, too relaxed to care if it's someone who's come to kidnap and torture me for their sociopathic pleasure.

Rico is already naked, stood in front of me wearing nothing but a smile and a gleam in his hooded eyes. He slides into the tub opposite me, causing the water to overflow, spilling it onto the marble-tiled floor. "Come here," he purrs, using one finger to motion me closer.

I do just that, spilling more water onto the floor as I turn, my back facing him when I slide between his muscled legs.

Heat pools from his body in glorious waves, puckering my skin. I'm on fire when I lean against his ripped torso, in heaven when he wraps his burly arms around me, holding me tight against him.

He manoeuvres himself so that he can massage my shoulders.

I can't even describe the sensations as his dexterous hands knead the knots from my body. Tilting my head back, I close my eyes, savoring every touch he delivers.

He reaches down, splaying his hands over the mounds of my breasts, before his fingers brush my nipples. He applies expert pressure to each, rubbing in circles, teasing me, calming me all at the same time. His lips find that sweet spot near the base of my neck, as his hands span out, then down, across my stomach, down toward the very core of me.

As his fingers disappear under the water, I follow his path with one of my hands, hovering over his as he finds my needy, hungry clit.

Using two fingers, he rubs with light strokes, playful, coaxing, leaving me begging for more as I arch my hips, gyrating them to encourage harder, faster movements. But he knows what he is doing; I feel him smile against my neck before he flicks his tongue out, tracing a hot, wet path up my flesh, tasting me before he sucks my earlobe between his teeth.

My body shivers, making waves in the water. I need more, so I turn into him, the water splashing around me. On my knees, I face him, weakened by the ravenous look he gives me from beneath his long, dark lashes.

Using my hands on the sides of the tub for support, I straddle him, hovering above him, enjoying the expectancy in his eyes for me to devour his long, stiff cock within the tight walls of my pussy.

As much as I want to prolong his torture, I can't. I need him inside me, more than I need the breath in my lungs. With the tip of him at my impatient entrance, I slide down, purposefully slow, feeling every swelling inch of his dick graze my insides to a point where his hardness is almost painful.

We both gasp, our lips parted, no other sound emitting, such is the intensity of the connection between us in this moment.

I rock my hips, back and forth, as he palms at my body, desperate to touch every inch, but unsure where to start or finish.

Clawing at my back, he scatters feverish kiss around my breasts, biting at the nipples, sending intense flashes of unabashed ecstasy through my veins at a million miles per hour.

I hold my breath as I feel the sudden onslaught of my climax rising from my depths, heating my core, deadening my limbs in the most beautiful way. Flutters in my stomach quicken, building up a crescendo of sexual gratification.

When they detonate, I grasp at Rico's shoulders, digging my nails into his flesh, burying my head in his neck where I bite at his skin, trying so hard not to hurt him, but not caring if I do all the same.

"Fuck." His engorged cock stretches me the more he swells inside me, sending my body into spasm, milking more from me than I thought possible.

When he comes, the ferocity of it takes me by surprise.

He swears out loud, gripping onto me, pumping everything he has into me as his body trembles against mine.

I barely register, when he lifts me out of the bath, carrying me in his arms toward the bed, where I sink, still damp, into the sheets, welcoming a dreamless sleep.

Chapter 9

We park the cars a good distance from the beach; somewhere inconspicuous – there's going to be a getaway vehicle waiting for us, to save time, so a couple of Dieter's guys will drive the cars away while we wait for the shipment to arrive.

We've got plenty of time ahead of ourselves to get prepared and in position.

Leo is somewhere on the beach, ensuring the transport is ready for us. He's also in a position to shoot, should anything unexpected happen.

Harris and Frankie – the sales team – are undercover on the beach, posing as rivals, ready to receive the shipment and start the fireworks.

Lucas is on comms. I can hear his voice coming through my earpiece as he talks to Dieter. The two of them are watching on monitors from the comfort of the villa.

There're a few other guns on the beach as back up. Me and Rico will be positioned better, away from the main action. We, too, can communicate with the guys, to make sure everyone keeps their eyes peeled and senses on high alert.

Despite the humidity in the air, my body shakes; whether from the cool sea breeze or the anticipation, I can't be sure, but I need to get it under control, or my aim is gonna be way off when the time comes. I don't normally suffer with nerves, even when there's a tight deadline to meet, but something about this whole situation I'm in isn't natural. Not to mention the fact, that I haven't been able to contact Warren about this – I'm out here on my own, so to speak. If something happens to me … well, I don't really wanna think about it.

Armed with our camouflaged duffles, and dressed in black, Rico and I head to where we're meant to be waiting for the boat to come in. We secure the spot, then set up the MSRs as we need them.

Fishing in my bag, I pull out my binos, giving the area a quick once over. It's quiet, no-one else around. Nevertheless, it does make me a little uneasy, that the original stretch of beach from last night is not too far away. Using the binoculars, I can make it out. I hope Dieter's not pissing in the wind when it comes to tactics. Seems a little too close to home for my liking.

Trying to ignore the impending doom crushing down on me, I look around the beach for the others. I spot a few hidden away in remote locations. There's no sign of Harris and Frankie yet, though; they'll be along with the rest of the rivals soon enough, I would imagine. We were always meant to be here first, to avoid detection as we set up.

I let out a deep, steading breath, crick my neck, then refocus my attention through the binos. "Head's up," I warn, spotting a vehicle coming across the sand.

"The twins?" Rico adjusts his sniper scope, zoning in on where I'm looking.

Yeah, I can see Harris and Frankie sat in the back of the topless jeep, bouncing around on the uneven ground, trying to maintain a hold of the guns close to their chests.

Rico lets everyone know by radio to get ready, stay quiet and hidden until the signal is given. "There's still a bit of waiting ahead of us." He checks his watch, lighting up the screen with an illuminous blue. "We've still got an hour to go."

An hour, with nothing but my anxiety, and a red-hot man to keep me company. Should be interesting.

"You're going to have to get in there quick when this goes down." Judging by Rico's dull tone of voice, he's still not best pleased that we've gotta steal off his boss.

To be honest, I'm not comfortable with him knowing that part, either, but I didn't have much of a choice. I *need* those drugs in order to give to Bruno. He has to know I have them for him, or he will torch that vital little piece of paper in front of me the very moment he suspects I'm lying. I have to produce the goods. "You know Dieter is going to get them back, though, right? It's only for show." Which is probably just as well, because I value my fingers in one piece, and exactly where they are.

"I know, but I'm still not comfortable with deceiving him like this." He turns to face me, his beautiful features highlighted by the pale moon. "We should have told him; he would have helped us."

Pfft, yeah, right. "I don't have that kinda time to risk, Rico, you know this. If we pull it off, then great, we can do some serious sucking up, if he even finds out that we borrowed some of his stash."

"You've met D, right?" His lips hitch into a nervous smile, that disappears just as quickly as it arrived. "I still think we could've gone about this differently."

"It is what is it," I remind him, not wishing to further discuss the bottomless hole I keep seeming to find myself digging for … well, myself.

"Where is this damn boat?"

I don't recognise the voice, but I know it's one of the men on the beach, as it's hushed, impatient.

"Keep your cool, Benny; we knew we had to wait this out for a bit." Rico is losing his patience, probably because he's sick of the wait, too, but it doesn't help to have idiots reminding you of it.

It's been barely ten minutes, and already we're starting to feel the pressure of the settling boredom.

"I'll need to create a distraction, otherwise I'm going to have to take what I need during transport." It's not the ideal topic of conversation to take Rico's mind off things, but it's all I've got. "Which means distracting a whole lot more people, loyal to Dieter, who have no idea of my situation like you do."

"We'll figure it out."

That's it? Well as a distraction technique, that sucked.

With a roll of my eyes, I pout my lips, sulking, before I take a quick look down my sniper scope. "Shit, look alive, guys." I radio through to those on the beach, as I spot the small silhouette of a fishing vessel come into focus. "They're early."

Through his attached earpiece, Rico utters, "Game on, boss."

Cussing and moaning come through my piece – for one's tired of waiting, they're sure kicking up a fuss at having to re-ready themselves for the unexpected.

From beside me, Rico whispers, "Wait for Frankie's signal; the moment he gives it, Asha takes out whoever's on the boat." He tilts his rifle at a slight downward angle. "I'll take the two in the jeep. Everyone else, lay down cover fire." He looks at me with a nod, which I return. "We're gonna need to act fast, the heat will be on us the moment someone reports gunfire."

I swallow hard. "Boat's drawing near," I advise, securing the suppressor to the end of my MSR.

Rico does the same. "How many?"

Squinting through my scope, I answer, "I see two…no, wait, make that three targets on the boat." I let out a breath, steady my angle and hover over the trigger. "I got the front two, Benny, I need you to take out the rear."

"Copy that."

The boat draws up to shore, where two of the three on board jump off. Frankie and Harris are already in the water, securing the vessel before they start offloading from it, and into the waiting jeep.

Before the two in the car can move, sirens send a screeching wail across the beach, flashing blue and red lights not far behind. Rico and I look at one another – wide-eyed.

"Fuck, what the hell?"

There's no time for a signal from anyone.

Guns are drawn as shouting and arguing erupt from the sand below.

Recalculating my distances, I squeeze the trigger and take the impact. My bullet sails – unseen – through the air and drives through the skull of one drug handler and into the second. They both land on their backs in the water with a splash, the other falls overboard as Benny releases his shot, dropping the third.

The two in the jeep, having turned their attention toward our position, catch bullets in the chest as Rico fires on them. Frankie and Harris are on it, heaving as much as they can between transports. Benny is heading down toward the jeep, tasked with throwing out the dead guys and driving Frankie, Harris and the drugs away.

The other two shooters – Tim and Jase – head down, too, while Rico puts his hand on my shoulder and nods toward the location where Leo is parked; hidden away in a nearby boat shed. We scramble up, gather our gear and make a run for it.

Benny is honking the horn, even as the twins are frantically loading the car. There's no way they'll get it all. Benny knows this, his patience is wearing thin again. He guns the jeep, spinning outta there, just as Frankie and Harris throw themselves into the seats. Of Tim and Jase, there is no sign.

Reaching the boat shed, the engine of the car thrums, vibrating against the wood-panelled floor. Leo's all ready to go, looking panicked, waving a frantic hand in our direction. We jump in as he says, “I’m not waiting. They’re almost on our asses.” He wheel spins outta the dilapidated warehouse, burning rubber until we’re a safe distance away.

I watch the jeep out of the back window, as it takes a different route. There goes my chance of getting what I needed. My heart sinks into the pit of my stomach.

Chapter 10

"What the fuck happened?" Dieter, red-faced and fuming, throws his glass of whiskey at the wall, where it obliterates into a million, shimmering pieces, making Lucas – who's sat next to him – and the rest of the team, jump. "Why were the fuckin' pigs there?"

"Th-they must've got wind boss," Rico stammers.

It's the first time I've seen him so blatantly lose his cool around his boss; he can normally hide it pretty well, but tonight, he's shook up. I think we all are. It's by some miracle that the boat turned up early enough for us to grab something. At least, a miracle for Dieter, not so much for me.

"I gathered that, you fuckin' genius, but how?" Dieter turns his glare one me. "Funny, how I take you on and then the shit hits the fan." His hand lingers over the gun tucked in his jeans. "Yesterday, you were conveniently in a car wreck, and tonight the cops are there with plenty of time to join the party before the time the boat should have actually shown."

Rico steps forward. "Hey—"

"Shut the fuck up," Dieter bellows. "Can you explain that to me, Asha?"

Straightening, and looking him dead in the eye, I answer, "No, boss. I'm not sure how you think I managed to cause a car wreck." Though, I did, but not on purpose. "Why would I want to risk my own life. There's a chance I could have died in that accident, so how would that have benefitted me? You have a mole, but it's not me—"

"She took two of Danny's men out, D."

Rico shuts up when Dieter glares at him, then back at me.

"Dead or alive, the cops could still have had us tonight. Maybe you think you're some kind of fucking martyr."

I don't take my eyes from him, and my voice doesn't quake when I tell him, "Your goons are sky-high at the best of times; letting girls get away to run their mouths. It's not that surprising that someone's caught a whiff. I'm not out to off myself over a small shipment of drugs; it wouldn't be worth my life."

Rico tenses beside me, and Dieter's hardened gaze bores into mine, nostrils flaring.

I've pissed him off, but what's the alternative? I've gotta keep rollin' with this, now. "Don't blame the new kid 'cuz your lackeys are developing loose tongues after they've been sniffing what you sell."

Dieter strides over to me, draws back his hand, then slaps me, hard.

I stand my ground, gaze remaining trained on him while I flex my jaw. He punches me this time, and I taste blood.

"All of you, out!" He addresses the room, then looks at me and Rico. "You two, stay."

My stomach sinks and Rico pales beside me; staring with slight fear behind his bulging eyes.

Once everyone's gone, Dieter takes a slow walk back behind his desk and sits, hands clasped on the surface in front of him. "First off," he mumbles, low, "don't *ever* talk to me like that again, Asha. Do you understand?"

I nod. "Sorry, boss. It won't happen again." I'm hoping I won't ever be put in another position like this for it to happen again. The guy punches like a pro-wrestler; my jaw still aches.

"I'll put a fuckin' bullet in your kneecap if it does." He lets out a heavy breath. "But you might be right. If I have rat, it needs flushing out."

"I have an idea, boss."

I turn to Rico, bewildered, and a little afraid of what he's going to say next. The look he gives me tells me it's exactly what I think it is. I want to shut him up, but if he plays this right, it might actually work in my favor, now.

"Asha's in some trouble with Bruno Martinez." He steps forward, taking a seat, offering me the one beside him.

"He's been threatening her to get him some top-quality shit."

"In exchange for what?"

I can tell Dieter is suspicious of the answer. He thinks I'm doing it for dirt on him. He'd be right, of course, but he doesn't need to know that. It's not what I told Rico, either.

"I want his contacts." It's my turn to chip in; I've gone over this story in my head a million times, so it's best coming from me. "I've been trying to get in with you guys for years, as you well know. I contacted Bruno with the false notion of taking you down, because I know how much you hate one another, when, in actual fact, I wanted his contacts for his trafficking ring to bargain my way into the Skull Caps with." I don't know if he's buying this, his face is expressionless and, now that I'm hearing it out loud, it is coming across a little far-fetched. "Bruno is small-time; I figured if I had something to give you that you didn't have, I'd earn points. But now, he knows I'm in and he wants me dead. He's just trying to see what else he can get from me before he blows my brains out."

"And how would Bruno have known about tonight?"

He doesn't believe me. He's got a point – Bruno would still have needed this information from someone, and I'm pretty sure I've made it look like that someone is me; possibly to try and save my own ass.

"Why don't we prove it?"

Dieter turns, slowly, toward Rico. He's getting more and more irate; a nerve is twitching in the side of his head. "*We,* is it?" He splays his fingers flat on his desk, rigid. "Tell me why the hell I should give a fuck, and why I shouldn't just shoot you in the head." He's turned his attention back to me now. "This is your mess, and you've brought your shit to my doorstep. What's stopping me popping a bullet between your eyes and delivering your carcass to Bruno, personally."

"Bruno's never gonna stop trying to get at you, boss."

"I didn't ask for *your* fucking opinion." Dieter uses his flat palms to push himself into a standing position. "I asked this bitch here." He nods his head in my direction, one hand going for his gun again, aiming it straight at me.

I can feel my bowels loosening, as I stare down the barrel. "Use me as bait, then." It's out there before I even know what I'm saying. "If you don't trust me, don't care if I live or die, then use me to get to him. What happens, happens." Two birds, one stone and all that.

Grabbing my hand, Rico leans into me. "What are you doing?" He's trying to be discreet, but it's difficult with Dieter looking at the pair of us.

"He doesn't trust me; maybe this will help. I don't wanna die, but it is my fault that Bruno is causing problems, so I should be used as whatever decoy is needed to take him out, once and for all." And hopefully, not die in the grisly process.

Dieter's mulling it over, I can tell by the intense glare he's giving me.

"It still might leave me with the potential problem of having a mole; if, indeed, it's not you."

"But it gets rid of a thorn in your side." I wish he would stop thinking of other excuses and just let me get on with this. This could be exactly what I need.

The shrill sound of Dieter's phone breaks the tension. He answers, a sternness still laced through his voice. Whoever is on the other end, is not making the mob boss happy. That vein in his head is racing, his teeth gritted. When he hangs up, he looks straight back at me, making me swallow, hard.

"We have another problem."

This cannot be good news for me. "What's wrong?" I almost didn't dare ask, but I kinda get the feeling he's expecting me to.

"That was Jase." His jaw is tense. "Tim's been shot and killed during the heist. He's been taken back to the fucking police headquarters." From off his table, he picks up another glass tumbler, launching this one at the wall, too. "He's a known fucking associate."

Oh, shit. I knew it, things are going from bad to worse, and I'm going to be leaving his house in a body bag before dawn. "You need to ditch the vehicles and move the dope."

The sting from the slap Dieter plants on my cheek, isn't as painful. I think my face is still numb from the first two hits.

"I fucking know that, you idiotic bitch. But this is one more problem *you're* causing me." He picks up his phone again, before I can even argue that statement. "Benny, grab the twins, burn the cars, shift the gear. You've got less than eight hours."

I want to ask him how he's deduced a time limit; I know that a search into known associates shouldn't take that long once they've ID'd Tim. Perhaps they have methods in place to delay identification; he clearly knows something I don't.

Hanging up, he puts his phone down, eyes closed, taking precious moments to collect himself before he faces the two of us, his eyes now open, piercing my very soul with the dark intent behind them. "Here's the deal. You take what you need from my stash, you go and see Bruno. Soon as you're in that bastards shit hole, in front of him, I'm having him waxed. Rico will go with you."

That last part might prove a little inconvenient, especially when I'm unexplainably rummaging through Bruno's pockets, looking for the list I could potentially be risking my life for. But there's little to no chance of me getting any sort of say in this. If I even dare to open my mouth in protest, Dieter will slice me open before I've even finished the sentence. All I can do is nod, and hope that I can think of something when the times comes.

*

I've left Rico at Dieter's mansion, told him I need some time to get ready. We can't both be seen going into Bruno's bar; it has to be me alone to begin with. I'm hoping I can use that opportunity to see where Bruno has the list stashed, then it might be a little easier to swipe it off him undetected.

First off, though, I have a bone of my own to pick. Fishing my phone from my holdall under the desk, I unlock it, look for the number I need, then hit the call button.

"Warren," a low drone answers.

"What the fuck, Tony?" I hiss. "You coulda gotten me killed, you asshole. What the hell kinda stunt did you think you were pulling?"

"I love it when you talk dirty to me, Evie." He's smiling – I can tell. Arrogant bastard.

"Fuck you, I'm serious. What was that shit? How the hell did you even know I was there?"

"When you were a no show the previous night, I--"

Anger takes hold of me. "I *knew* that was you. I told you to leave off."

"Evie." His tone takes on a more serious note. "You're not heading up the investigation into his drug ring. I am. And when I didn't hear from you by our deadline, I had someone look into your whereabouts. And, I might add, that you're lucky I did, because you were admitted into hospital under your real name."

"What?" I don't know whether I'm angry at him for having someone spy on me, or a little afraid that someone else might also know my real identity and use it against me. Either way, the dozy bastard still just doesn't understand what it could have cost me. "I get that, Tony. But it was too obvious. New girl arrives, suddenly the cops know every move the Skull Caps make. Dieter blamed me for you guys showin' up tonight, and thinks that yesterday's accident was some kind of game play."

"Blamed?"

Typical. Ignore all the other shit I said. "Somehow, I managed to bullshit my way out of it, but that doesn't mean that I'm off the hook. He still doesn't trust me, and, now, because of that, I've gotta get involved in more of his shit to prove myself." I let out a deep breath. "As if the Marco job wasn't enough, now I've gotta put my life on the line again, and all because you just couldn't take me at my word." It's a little disheartening, considering the history Warren and I share … shared. "Stop tailing me; you're going to get me outed."

"What's the job?"

I can't exactly tell him the whole thing. He knows what he needs to know, but he doesn't know about my hidden agenda; the real reason I've been sucking up to Bruno. If he knew, he'd take me off the case, tell me I'm being reckless, that I can't be involved because it's a conflict of interest. Well, bullshit to that. I need answers. I need my revenge for what Dieter did to me and my family two years ago. Warren doesn't know it was Dieter, but I did my research before I volunteered to be in on the mission to quash his drugs ring. It's not the only thing I'm going to put an end to.

"You don't need me to tell you. You'll have me followed, regardless." I hang up the phone.

On top of everything else, I now need to find a way of getting out of the hotel unseen. I need to think where Warren might post men to keep an eye on me. Considering I know most of their faces, they'll be concealed pretty damn good.

Chapter 11

There's no way of telling where Warren has men stationed, watching over me. I'm just going to have to take the most inconspicuous route I can think of, and hope for the best.

I hide the drugs Dieter gave me in the inside pocket of my cotton jacket. My Glock goes in the concealed holster on the opposite side, along with a small pocket pistol tucked into my boot, hidden by the bottom of my pants. One can never be too cautious. I usually carry a blade there, but guns are quicker and less messy.

Locking my room behind me, I head downstairs, toward the kitchens. I've been here long enough for the staff to know my face, so they don't say anything to me when I walk through, making my way to the door that leads to the back alleyway. Something sure smells good, though, and it reminds me, I haven't eaten in a while. I'll grab something after. If I eat now, and shit goes down the way it's supposed to, I'll probably end up bringing it back up, either from running around, ducking and diving, or the adrenaline after things go quiet. Not something I fancy, either way.

I tip-toe my way up the alley. Lord only knows why; there's thousands of different noises all around that easily conceal my footsteps. I'm on the look-out for any vehicles parked nearby with their drivers still sat in them, or someone hanging around outside a café or bar, pretending to read a newspaper, but glancing toward the hotel entrance every now again when they think no-ones looking.

I just need to make it to the next alley without being seen, then I can openly walk the streets away from the hotel without the risk of being caught.

A rusted, battered van pulls up in front of me, as I'm about to enter the next alleyway. The side doors slide open, two men in balaclavas jump out, grab me, then force me into the van. I try to scream, kick out, only one has a grubby, fishy-smelling hand wrapped around my mouth. All I want to do instead, is hurl at the taste. The other grabs my legs and between them, they chuck me into the van, unceremoniously, slamming the door behind them when they climb in.

My heart races as I look at the dirty faces of the two Puerto-Ricans in my line of sight, from my position on my stomach on the floor of the now-moving vehicle.

One of them boots me in the thigh, causing me to cry out at the dull thud that reverberates through my lower extremities.

Son of a bitch will pay for that.

The other – while I'm still reeling from the agony – hauls me up by the neck of jacket, then tapes my hands together in front of me with grey gaffer tape.

I have an urge to headbutt the fucker, but that won't do me any good in my current situation. I open my mouth to hurl verbal abuse at him instead, only he tapes that, too.

Given that I can't lash out, nor swear my disapproval at the two men in the van with me, I take the time to survey my surroundings. I can't see much out of the back windows; they're covered in what looks like years' worth of oil and excrement … smells like it, too. We're heading away from the main streets, though, that much I can tell. The buildings are becoming less and less, replaced by blue sky and the occasional telephone pole.

I recognise the two men. It took me a moment, but I can place their faces at Bruno's bar, usually sat downstairs smoking questionable cigarettes, playing poker or dominos. No doubt the driver is also a friend of these delinquents.

When they talk to one another, it's in their native language. I don't speak Porta Rican, and if it weren't for the fact that I have tape covering my mouth, I'd tell them not to be so damn rude, to speak English so that I can get involved in their conversation. Or, at least try to decipher where they're taking me.

Right now, Warren's spies would be a welcome sight. Right now, I'm actually preying that one of them saw what happened.

The van comes to a stop. The doors are opened, then I'm hauled out just as brusquely as when I was thrown in. I can't even get my shit together enough to plant my feet firmly on the ground. Instead, I'm dragged by these two asshats, their arms under mine, feet scraping through the dust-covered floor, to a rickety, wooden chair in the middle of a rundown warehouse.

Dumping me into the chair, the two men walk off to my right, knocking on the door of a small office I've only just noticed.

Out walks Bruno, a cigar in his mouth, a gun in his hand.

"Well, well," he drones, his thick lips twitching with stifled joy, "what do we have here? Looks like a deer caught in headlights." Strolling up to me, he smashes his fist into my face.

The chair rocks on unsteady legs, but somehow, remains upright, with me still on it.

When Bruno rips the tape off my mouth, I find my voice. "You bastard." For hitting me, and for taking off a few layers of skin with that damn tape. I flick my tongue out to wet my dry lips, tasting that familiar copper tang.

“You have something for me.” It’s not a question.

“And I’d have given it to you myself, without a fight. You didn’t need to send the welcome committee.” I spit blood onto the floor, in the opposite direction of Bruno’s expensive moccasins. “Am I to assume that our deal has changed slightly?”

Laughing, he tells me, “You assume correct.” He gets right up into my face, close enough that I can smell the cigar, feel the heat from it on my own lips. “You see, I know who you are.”

My blood runs cold. Despite having all the training in the world, I know that my face just gave away my reaction, because his knowing smile widens.

“I know why you want this.” He pulls the coveted list from his breast pocket, before taking the cigar out of his mouth. He hands them both to one of his goons. “Look after these a second, will ya?”

The next punch he gives me, does knock me off the chair. I try to use my restrained hands to soften the fall, but I’m still winded when I hit the hard concrete.

Bruno turns me over, placing a foot either side of me as he uses one hand to tug me up by my lapels. The other delivers another blow, vibrating painfully through my jaw. By the time he sends the third smashing into my cheek, I am on the verge of losing consciousness. The pain is dizzying.

"Stay with me, princess," he taunts, dropping me to the ground.

My face aches. I close my eyes against it, willing it to all be a dream. Hoping that, after coming this far – seeing what I need only an arm's length away – that it doesn't all come crashing to an end within the next few, valuable moments.

Who am I kidding? I'm outnumbered, trussed up like a hog, half-dazed without a hope or a prayer that I'm gonna make it out of this alive.

Twisting my body back onto the side, I try to use my hands to dig into my inside pocket. *Last chance.*

But Bruno sees me, orders his men to shove me back in the chair, where he rifles through my pockets. He pulls out the drugs with a triumphant smile, then delves back in, purposely molesting my breasts before he finds my Glock. He stashes my gun in his waistband, then snaps his fingers.

His goon comes over, handing him back his cigar and the piece of paper I so desperately want.

"I don't think you're going to find what you're looking for." He brings the cigar closer to my list. "Knowing Dieter, the way I do, whoever you're trying to find, is likely dead and buried."

The thought makes me retch. But when he sets the paper on fire, it's all I can do not to be sick. My stomach is convulsing, tears are pouring down my battered face. Everything I have worked for, everything I have risked has just gone up in flames. The absolute, bottomless feeling of desolation that surges through me, is like nothing I have ever felt before in my life. Not even when we got the news that my sister was missing, presumed dead … even then, I still clung on to some degree of hope. But I'm watching that hope burn, I'm watching the orange embers eat away at the only reason I still exist. I close my eyes, allowing myself to be drowned in the tears I have kept in for two years.

When I hear the click of my gun, feel the cold metal pressed against my forehead, I know I am ready to welcome death.

A shot rings through the warehouse, the gun falls away from my head before I hear a thud.

Opening my eyes, I see Bruno on the ground, a bullet wound seeping dark liquid from between his eyes. His cronies are scrambling for their own weapons, aiming them somewhere behind me, firing off shot after shot.

A stray bullet catches me in the shoulder, buries itself in my body. The impact catapults me off the chair, sending me skidding across the floor. Looking up, I see Rico behind some boxes, his smoking gun aimed at the guys beside me, both on their backs, dead, eyes open, glazed, staring at me as though I'm their killer.

Rushed footsteps echo through the building. Rico drags me to my feet, takes my weight against him as my body slumps. Whether from the bullet wound, or the will to live seeping through my skin, I don't know. He shouts at me to pull myself together, but I can't; I don't have the strength to anymore.

Two more men enter the warehouse, panic on their faces as they look behind them, hoping that the wail of sirens I hear aren't as close as they're fearful of. Between two of them, they get me to the waiting car. The other jumps behind the wheel, waiting for the doors to close before he speeds off.

*

The throbbing in my shoulder, when I wake, feels like someone is pounding the muscle from the inside with twelve, steel, lump hammers. To top that off, it feels like someone is sitting on my face with a concrete ass. My jaw hurts like a son of a bitch; I wonder if it's broken at all.

"You're awake."

Despite the pain, I smile through it when I hear Rico's voice. Turning my head, I see him sitting up, alert, in a chair beside me. He looks afraid to come near me and touch me.

"I'm OK," I assure him, realising now that talking is bad idea. It's like I'm reliving each punch with every word. I screw my face up, only to find that that also causes me fresh pain.

"We had the doc take a look at you." Rico stands, walks closer, but still looks wary of touching me. "It's gonna hurt for a bit, but he's left some strong meds to take some of the edge of."

Strong meds to take the edge off? That leaves me slightly perturbed as to what is exactly in those meds.

"Don't worry, they're just painkillers."

Either he's psychic, or my face betrayed me, again. Regardless, I look around my close proximity, desperate for these drugs. I can't go through the rest of the day not being able to voice my opinion to people – how will I cope? How will I be able to quench my growing hunger if I'm not able to munch on a cheeseburger. I better not have to live on *soup* for the foreseeable future. I hate soup. And soup isn't even worth the effort if it hasn't got bread with it, which puts me right back at square one.

Rico grabs some pills from the bedside drawer beside me, then heads to the en suite to pour me a glass of water.

Pointless; I've already swallowed the tablets in my desperation before he even returns. I can't imagine trying to drink is going to be any less painful than speaking, so I'm not risking it. I hope they kick in soon; I'm famished. My stomach grumbles with a loud groan.

"I'll fetch you something soft to eat. I think D has some soup in the refrigerator."

I murmur my disapproval, hoping that he gets the message that I am *not* touching soup. I'd rather starve. Shaking my head when Rico looks at me hurts like hell, but I'll ride it out this once, if it means no damn soup passes my lips.

“You have to eat something, babe.” He walks back toward me, sitting down again.

“Not soup.” Ah, they’re kicking in quite quickly, that wasn’t nearly as painful as last time. “I *detest* soup.”

The smile he gives me lights up the room, making me feel better for having had to endure a little bit of agony just to tell him that. I try to return his smile, though it feels crooked as I test my pain threshold. Oh well, he knows I mean well.

“How about we take a picnic down to the beach then? But I’m looking for easy food; nothing fancy.”

The grin on my face grows. I didn’t even know he possessed such a romantic side to him. It’s endearing; especially considering I didn’t think I could be floored by romance anymore. I thought most of my emotions were null and void. I nod my acceptance, butterflies prancing around like twats on speed in my belly.

Within an hour, I’ve numbed myself on enough painkillers to be able to get dressed. The thudding, both in my skull and my shoulder, are down to dull aches; tolerable enough to spend a couple of hours doing nothing but relaxing on the beach.

Dieter hasn't said much to me since we got back from the warehouse. He's not really looked at me all that much, either. I'm hoping he's beginning to believe that I'm on his side. Between a car crash and a bullet, there's no way he can think that I'd happily risk my life to such extents just to see him go under. In a way, he's right. I'm not risking everything just to watch him get a few years for drug peddling. I want to watch him fry for what he's being doing to young, innocent girls for years. I've seen the pictures of them, alive and dead, their bodies battered – sometimes beyond recognition – used in ways you could only hear about from the most sick and twisted minds. Sold to the most evil, degrading, vile pigs you could imagine, abused for a couple of years until they come of age, then shot and buried in the middle of nowhere, with little hope of their families ever finding them again.

I swallow back the bile scratching at my dry throat, try to hold back the hot tears stinging the corners of my eyes, holding on to the last shred of hope I have that my sister didn't meet such a gruesome end at the hands of these monsters.

In the car next to me, Rico puts a hand on my thigh while he drives. "You're so beautiful," he murmurs, with a sparkle of lust behind his eyes.

He clearly missed the torment that plagues me every hour of every day. I'm thankful for that; if he'd have started asking questions, I wouldn't have been able to hold in my tears. It's like those moments when you're being eaten away at from the inside, but on the outside, everything's roses and unicorns – a façade to fool those into thinking you're getting on with life … until that moment when someone asks if you're OK, and the floodgates flip a switch that you don't have any control over. You try to nod, hum an incoherent yes, but at the same time, your bottom lip trembles and your eyes give you away, before the tears come in inconsolable waves.

I can only manage a small smile, wondering what's come over him all of a sudden.

We pull up to a secluded stretch of beach, made all the more serene by the paling sun against a background of stunning pinks and yellows, melting into one another across the fading sky. There's still a welcome warmth in the air, mingled with the scent of the cooling sea breeze, It's perfect.

Taking my hand, Rico pulls me toward the golden sands. Waves lap at the shoreline in a mesmerising, provocative dance, ending in sparkling, foaming sprays at our feet, as we walk through it, toward a more remote area, hidden by large rock formations.

He seats me down on a flat slab of stone.

It's warm against my skin. I close my eyes, savoring the sensations, groaning when I feel Rico's soft lips against my own. When he slips his tongue into my mouth, I growl, running my fingers through his hair, over his shoulders, pulling his huge, muscled body closer to me.

He parts from me, placing his cheek against mine. "I want to make love to you, Asha." His easy tone tickles the skin of my neck, giving me goosebumps.

Inside, I am screaming, both for happiness and sadness. Rico cannot be falling in love with me, nor can I be falling for him. He is a criminal; I am an undercover, federal agent. Falling for this man goes against everything I stand for. He works for the man who defiled my sister, because she refused to sleep with other men to line his pockets. That thought alone should be enough to make my skin crawl.

But Rico has gotten under my skin. He is not the man Dieter is. He's not cold or calculating. He's warm, passionate, romantic. He makes me feel things I thought were dead and buried. I am in love with him. I am in love with a criminal.

It scares me, to be standing so very close to the edge of destruction, yet, I cannot help myself.

Through my inner turmoil, a groan rumbles in my chest as Rico cups my breast in his large, warm hand, tweaking the nipple between thumb and forefinger. The breath catches in my throat and, despite the ache, I arch further into his touch.

His tongue glides into my mouth, stroking my own, moistening my lips, fuelling the fire burning deep inside me like a raging fever.

When we part, I gasp for breath.

He unzips my jeans, sliding them down my legs, over my calves. His smooth hands caress my thighs when he kisses his way back up, before removing his own pants. Kneeling before me, his hot breath sweeps across my damp core. "I can't draw this out, babe. I want you so fuckin' bad; I need to be inside you, now."

He waits, as though he is waiting for my permission, afraid that if he lets his carnal urges free, he will hurt me. I nod my head once, parting my legs for him, inviting him in.

Lifting himself over me, with one, slow, deep movement, he impales me with his thick length. He fills me completely, hugging my tight walls with every inch of his engorged shaft.

My cry of pleasure is drawn out, as I dig my nails into the taut skin of his sculpted shoulders. When he draws out, the sweet friction sends me into a tailspin. I quiver against him, biting my bottom lip.

Looking deep into my eyes, he slides into me again. Slow; gloriously slow, so that I can feel every inch of his magnificent cock as it hits the back of me, stretching me, satisfying my every need.

His languid movements – purposeful and raw – gyrate against my sweet spot, making my body tremble beneath him. I lose myself behind an orgasmic haze; climbing higher and higher until my body feels like it's floating. I clench myself, tight around his swollen member, feeling him rub the sides of my slick entrance. Somewhere, jumbled words float through me…

Feel ... good ... Ev ... so g ... lov ... way ... el

I am lost when heat pools in my stomach, as my toes curl. My skin prickles, flushes hot the moment I let go, crashing around him. I milk his cock, tightening around the length, feeling him pulsate and swell inside me before he, too, releases his jet of hot fluid into me.

Chapter 12

My days recovering, are mostly spent in bed with Rico. Dieter hasn't turfed me out, yet, which I'm taking as a good sign. He's even asked how I'm feeling … once … via Rico, and it was more of a, "she's not dead, yet, then," kinda question. Even so, the fact that I'm still here, bodes well for me.

When every shred of hope I had, went up in flames with that list, my very being died on the spot. But, I've been given some time to think about how I can work this in my favor. I mean, I'm already in the lion's den, so to speak. He doesn't trust me fully, but nothing else has happened, so far. I'm hoping it's swaying him back in my favor. Maybe I can even blame it on the dead Tim, in time, when Dieter and I are back on speaking terms.

I've been asking Rico what jobs are coming up. He's reluctant to let me get involved, given my injured state, but I'm able to do some things, I've reassured him. Even if it means sitting at a computer with Lucas, using my eyes and my mind, instead of my body. I'll be out of the line of fire then, too. Good news for Rico's peace of mind, not so agreeable with Dieter's desire to see me dead.

There is one thing I need to do, though. I need to get in touch with Warren. He hasn't heard from me in days. He might have guys staked out near the house, but that's assuming he knows what happened at the warehouse, as well as my current location. I won't know until I'm able to talk to him. To do that, I need to prise Rico from my side long enough to get back to the hotel, retrieve my phone, and give him a call.

Sitting up in bed, I glance over at the clock. It's still early, but the sun is up.

The bedroom door opens. Rico strolls in with a tray that smells like I'm going to be thanking him before I actually move from this spot.

"I made bagels." He smiles, triumphantly.

By made, he means he popped them under the grill before adding cream cheese and bacon. I still thank him, as does my grumbling stomach.

Eating has become easier over the last few days. Nothing's broken in my jaw, but I did take quite the beating. It's healing now, and the meds are still taking the edge off when I need them to.

"I was thinking, I need to get back to the hotel." I've got a mouthful of bacon, but neither one of us cares. "I've overstayed my welcome, and I'm pretty sure Dieter still doesn't know whether he wants me here, or not."

"I'll come with you."

Shit. How am I meant to ring Warren if Rico is hanging around? "You don't have to do that; I know Dieter's got you working a few jobs. I don't want to be a distraction for you, give him another excuse to hate me."

Rico puts down his bagel. "Dieter doesn't hate you."

"Oh, pull the other one, Rico. He still doesn't trust me, and would just as rather shove me off a balcony than let me in on another job." I shrug my shoulders. "I'm just hanging around doing nothing. It's not what I signed on for."

"I'll speak with him today, see if you can do something light, something to ease you back in. Maybe even from here, so he can keep his eye on you; know that you're not up to anything."

"I still need to get back and grab my things." I roll my eyes at him. "I can't keep wearing just your shirts, Sirus is starting to look at me like he's a rabid dog, and I'm a prime piece of bloodied steak."

Growling, Rico launches himself at me, nibbling at my neck. "Oh, but you are. My steak, to devour whenever I want."

His animal reaction sends shivers up and down my spine.

Rico throws the empty tray off the bed, rips off his t-shirt, then ravages me in every way a man should.

*

Rico's sleeping after fucking me senseless for the past three hours.

Careful not to wake him, I climb out of bed, slipping into my unwashed jeans, and another of Rico's shirts. This one's a little smaller than the rest, and slightly more feminine. Perhaps it belongs to one of the floozies I see milling around here. So long as it's her just her shirt in Rico's bedroom, and not her, we won't have any issues.

Rico won't be happy to find me gone when he wakes up, but I can't risk having him at the hotel while I make the call to Warren. It's not going to be one of those quick, two minute catch up calls. I've been AWOL for days, he's going to chew me a new one, demand to know what I know, and why I've been off the radar. That's assuming he doesn't have any clue about what went down at the warehouse. That's gonna open up a whole bunch of other questions I won't be inclined to answer. Maybe I actually am safer staying here.

I know that isn't true.

Making my way downstairs, I'm hoping there aren't too many people around to question what I'm doing, sneaking around the house without my bodyguard. Not that I owe them any answers.

Just my luck, that Dieter is walking out of his office just as I reach the front door. "Going somewhere?" He raises one brow, stood still, hands behind his back as he waits for my response.

"I need to get back to the hotel. All my stuff is there." I loosely fondle the material of Rico's shirt, just to make a point. "I'll be back tonight." Or will I?

"Where's Rico?"

Oh, this is ridiculous. "He's upstairs, asleep. I don't need him to escort me everywhere." Despite things being tenuous between Dieter and I, I still cannot seem to hold my tongue around him. Sometimes, even *I* question whether or not I've got a death wish. "He's tired, and he's working tonight; he needs the rest. I won't be gone long."

His glare unnerves me, it's as though he's pondering over something. Probably which way would be best to kill me. "Fine, be back by nine. I want you watching the feed with Lucas tonight."

Eyes wide, I do a double-take of the mob boss. "Excuse me?"

"You heard me, don't act like a prick. Nine. Last chance." He walks off toward the kitchen.

Dumbfounded, I find the door handle, opening it, letting myself out into a warm afternoon. I'm going to walk a little way, until I see a cab I can hail. The sun feels good on my skin, like I haven't had my daily dose of vitamin D since being shot, and it's taking the opportunity to soak into my flesh.

I also want to think about what tonight means. What will I be watching? Rico hasn't really told me much about what he's been doing for the last few days. I assume, more of the same, but I really don't know. Perhaps I'm going to be watching over the next drug heist. Dieter hasn't said anything more about the last lot, but I gathered from others that he needed to sell fast and cheap, making a loss because of it. It wouldn't surprise me if he needed to take on more jobs just to make the money back.

I wave my hand out when I see a cab. When it stops, I climb in, instructing the driver to take me to my hotel. It isn't too far from where I am, but I can't keep putting off the inevitable. I need to call Warren with an update.

Someone's been in my room. The air conditioning is off, and I always switch it on before I leave. With soaring temperatures outside, it's usually the safest bet to avoid immediate dehydration upon entering the room. Someone has definitely been here while I've not been.

Rushing toward my desk, I look under it for my holdall. It's still there, but it's been tampered with. The pockets are half unzipped. Fishing through it, I'm relieved to see that my phone is still in the same place I left it. Turning it over in my hands, it looks OK. The back is still glued closed, stopping someone from opening it and bugging me. I have several locking mechanisms that need to be bypassed before someone can access the content.

I put in my pin code, then use the fingerprint recognition software to unlock the screen. I have over seventy-five missed calls, and almost as many voicemails. Swiping through, I can see that they're all from Warren. I'm not going to listen to each and every one, I'll be here too long. I only listen to the last one. It's Warren, informing me that he's located me and has me under surveillance.

I better call him; though, the likelihood is, that he knows I've returned to the hotel already. Nevertheless, it doesn't hurt to be courteous.

Hitting the call button on his number, I brace myself for the onslaught of verbal abuse I'm going to receive.

"Jesus H Christ, Evie, tell me that's you." There's genuine concern in Warren's urgent tone.

"It's me." I take a seat on the edge of my bed. "I couldn't call; I've been holed up at Dieter's. He still doesn't trust me." I remember why, now. "And that's your fucking fault, Tony, remember?" I know I'm the one who should be getting my ass handed to me, but I'm in this shitstorm of a situation because of my boss. "I've risked my life for this damn assignment, more than once. Please start trusting that I know what I'm doing. You're jeopardising my safety."

"Can I talk?" Typical, disregards everything I've said.

I wait in silence, not really feeling up to giving him my nod of approval, so to speak.

"I should have trusted you, and I'm sorry. I know you've had to do some … unsavory things to get where you are right now." *He does?* "I saw the warehouse, saw Martinez. I know you were shot; your blood was at the scene, and I recovered your gun."

Ah shit, I knew I shouldn't have underestimated the basics of forensic training. "Tony, don't ask me to explain what I was doing there. I can't tell you."

"Your blood isn't the only thing we found, Evie." Warren doesn't sound mad, he sounds … pitying almost. "There was a charred piece of paper."

My world comes crashing in around me once again, with the stark reminder that everything I have done, every life I've taken, could all soon be for nothing. If Warren knows what's on there, he'll drag me back in, reassign me, and then everything goes out the window.

"It's been analysed," he continues, bringing me back down to earth, "and there were names on that list. Missing girls from two years ago. Evie, what are you doing?"

I can't hold it in any longer. The weight bearing me down, the hopelessness in my heart, the loss gut-punching me twenty-times over. It all comes out in a torrent of tears. Placing my head in my free hand, I sob.

Pulling myself together, I beg Warren, "Let me finish what I started."

"You know I can't do that, Evie. Once word gets out about the list, your whereabouts, shit's gonna roll downhill." He still has that same hint of sympathy laced in his words.

"Buy me some time. Twenty-four hours." My voice is less shaky, more determined now to settle what I started out to. "I'm on a job tonight, at least let me scope it out. If it's small, I'll walk away. If it's big, we take him down. Twenty-four hours, please, Warren. You owe me this." In all fairness, he probably doesn't owe me jack shit, but he has put my life on the line, so I think I'm entitled to one, small favor. He doesn't need to know that, if tonight doesn't deliver what I'm preying for, then I'll go dark until I find it.

He's taking his time giving me an answer, making me feel sicker the longer I'm left waiting.

"Twenty-four hours, and I want an update the moment you know what's going on." It's with a lot of pent up frustration that he agrees to my timeline, I can hear the exasperation in his voice. "I mean it, Evie. At the moment, I can play this off as the drugs bust it was always intended to be, with a little bonus if we get it, but the moment you start going rogue, forgetting about the drugs, then we're both done for. And I will not lose my job for you." He pronounces the last statement quite matter-of-factly. "Do you understand?"

"Yes." I don't care as much as I should, but that doesn't mean I don't understand what he's saying. "Oh, someone's been in my room." I should probably let him know that, just in case we're being listened to, or watched.

"It was me." He's calm about that fact, not once thinking to mention it to me before now. "I wanted to see if anything had been compromised; we're good. Twenty-four hours." He hangs up on me, leaving me both a little pissed, but also relieved.

Grabbing my bag, other guns, and stashing my phone in the gusset of my panties – for safe-keeping and to avoid detection, of course – I head down to the lobby, call a cab, then wait for it to take me back to Dieter's.

Chapter 13

The drive back is a little more relaxed than earlier. That is, until I pull up outside. I'm fully aware that I have a mobile telephone stashed in my delicates, that, if found, will most certainly sign my death warrant. Rico isn't usually in the habit of coping a feel like an inexperienced, horny teenager, but, let's face it, my luck hasn't been all that solid as of late. I'm going to have to remove it as soon as possible and hide it somewhere secure … in a mob boss's house, that I'm not familiar with. Perfect.

The front door opens as I walk toward it. Sirus grins at me from inside the foyer. "Saw you pull up."

Great, what do you want, a fucking certificate? The way he's ogling me, it's like he thinks he's doing me favor, acting the gentleman by opening the door. One could surmise he's after more than a certificate for his good deed of the day.

"Outta my way, Sirus. Where's Rico?" I don't have time for his lechery. Plus, he *is* likely to grope me like an inexperienced, horny teenager. I don't think Dieter would appreciate me slicing one of his guys from stomach to sternum right now.

Sirus steps away from the door. If looks could kill, my throat would be shredded.

I don't know why he's so pissed; he knows Rico and me have a thing going. He can't honestly believe I'd give up Rico for *him.* He's a disgusting barbarian, usually chasing skirt at least twenty years young than my thirty-four. I can't stand him; I look forward to the day that I get to bury him – literally, six foot in the ground.

Without an answer, I make my way upstairs, back toward the bedroom Rico and I have claimed as ours. There's an en suite, and I'm hoping there's a concealed place for me to dump this phone until I need it.

Rico is there, waiting on the edge of the bed.

"You're back?" He doesn't sound overly pleased, but that's likely because I left him without a word this morning.

"Yeah, sorry I didn't wake you. I knew I wasn't going to be long, and you looked peaceful." I try to smile through the awkward moment, hoping he doesn't notice how uncomfortable I am, desperate for him – for once – not to touch me before I can make it to the bathroom.

Standing, he strolls over to me, casual, calm. "I missed you."

For the first time ever, the look in his eyes unnerves me. The fluttering in my stomach isn't from lust-fuelled butterflies, but instead, a kind of sickness. Is it because I know he will more than likely talk me into bed? If he does, he will find my phone, and I can't allow that to happen. At the same time, if I act in any way out of the ordinary, he's going to get suspicious.

My body is starting to tremble, my brain whirring through excuses, lies, any kind of tangible plan that will come across as feasible.

He snakes his arms around me, drawing me close for a kiss, caressing down my back toward my ass, which he cups.

I try to swallow, but my throat is dry. He's too close. I knew my luck would run out sooner or later; he's going to try and molest me in all the right places … but at such a wrong, wrong time.

"Rico," I murmur, my voice a little husky. "I need to go to the bathroom; I think mother nature has arrived early." He'll know what that means, right? He'll buy that, surely. Men get squeamish around this kinda talk, don't they?

With a kiss to my forehead, he lets me go. "You best go and see." He winks at me.

It takes a monumental effort to keep in the heavy sigh of relief that's eager to get out. I kiss his lips, then walk right by him, heading for the bathroom. Locking the door behind me, I lean against it, letting out a long breath. I'm still shaking when I drop my pants, fishing the phone out of my underwear. I can't wait for this to all be over.

Searching the en suite as I pull my jeans up, I try to find somewhere where I don't think anyone would look. There're no loose tiles, or any wood coming away from anything. *Shit,* this is going to be difficult.

The cabinets are no good, people go through bathroom cabinets all the time. There's limited storage space, but even that wouldn't be too clever, either. I don't have anything waterproof to put it in, so that I could leave it in the tank. *Think, Evie, think.* Time is running out, Rico will soon be wondering what's taking so damn long.

The light fixture. Above me, the lighting is a sturdy, decorative piece that's box shaped. The design is metal, so I could leave it on top of there, and no one would see it, even with the light on.

Grabbing the wooden box used for laundry, I climb onto it, steadying myself in case it topples. Reaching toward the fixture, I place the phone on top. The light sways slightly, but soon comes to a stop.

I get down, replace the laundry box, flush the toilet – for good measure – then vacate the bathroom, but not before kicking off my jeans, leaving them in there.

"False alarm." I grin at Rico – now lying on the bed – trying to force my body to stop shaking from the adrenaline. "Where were we?" Using both hands, I grab the bottom of my top, lifting it over my head. I purposely didn't wear a bra, and it's proving an awesome distraction technique.

Rico's eyes widen, one brow raised. He licks his lips, then removes his own t-shirt, discarding it on the floor alongside mine. Grabbing for my waist, he hauls me onto the bed. He's still got that fire in his eyes, only now, it's turning me on, not off.

I want to have a little fun with him, before he fucks me stupid.

Hovering above him, I give him my best chaste smile, before I dip my head down, snaking out my tongue to lick his dark nipples. He smells so good; like cocoa butter and almonds. Traipsing kisses down his taut body, I use one hand to finger the waistband of his underwear, the tips skimming his erection as it pulses under the confines of the material.

He groans, knowing what I plan to do him, as he lifts his hips while at the same time, shimmying his briefs down, around his ankles where he kicks them away.

I tilt my head to look at him from under my long lashes, the corners of my lips hitching into a smile. I enjoy the shameless look of lust in his chocolate eyes, the glint in them as he lowers his gaze, urging me to follow with my mouth. I oblige him; taking his thick cock in one hand, gripping, watching his eyes close, as my tongue laps up his excitement. I know he wants to be in my mouth, almost as much as I want him there, but the temptation to tease him with the power I now hold, is too much.

Splaying my other hand across his defined abs, I dig my nails in – not too hard, just enough to make him open his eyes. He watches my tongue as I wrap it around his head, savoring the taste of him, my own excitement dampening the thin, lacy material of my panties. I draw him deeper into my open mouth.

He hisses, expecting me to close my lips around him, his heightened frustration verbally apparent when I don't. "Jesus Christ, Asha, I want to fuck your mouth so hard." His teeth are gritted together, his body tense, one hand fisting the duvet beneath him, the other fumbling, twitching, desperate to grab the back of my head and force me down on his dick.

He doesn't, though. He enjoys the salacious torment every bit as much as I do.

The longer I play with him inside my open mouth, the closer his hand gets to my head. He rests it on his thigh, his fingers gripping his own flesh, leaving red marks. His balls tighten with every throb of his delicious cock.

I close my lips around him, sucking him in as deep as he will go, my tongue still stroking his shaft, hand moving up and down in time with my head as I draw him in, out, in, murmuring my desire against his length, the vibrations hardening him all the more.

He moves the hand on his thigh across, weaving his fingers through my hair.

His grip on me is hard; somewhere between pleasure and pain, but I find it fucking hot. I'm wet at the thought of having so much dominance over one being, someone so masculine, so dangerous, so … alpha. This man – whose hands have ended the life of so many – is at my mercy, and nothing is more arousing to me in this moment, then watching him, helpless against me as I make him succumb to me, using only my mouth.

A knock at the door makes him jump.

Thankfully, his dick is mostly out of my mouth, so the risks of him choking me were gratefully reduced. It doesn't stop me rolling my eyes, however, desperate to decapitate the inconsiderate asshole who's interrupted what could have been a gratifying situation.

"Fuck off," I shout, once Rico is completely out of my mouth, "we're busy in here." I couldn't give a flying fuck who it is, nor if they've cottoned on to what we were up to. My frustration knows no bounds, nor does it have a filter.

Rico chuckles, lifting himself up and off the bed, heading toward the door, still naked.

His ass is sculpted perfection; the distraction almost making me forget that I, too, am in a state of undress. Jumping under the covers, I pull the duvet up to cover my modesty, my sensitive nipples grazing the silky fabric, making me shudder.

Rico opens the door a fraction, keeping the majority of what I enjoy most about him, out of plain sight.

"Dieter wants you both downstairs, now."

Sirus. That fucking idiot is beginning to become the bane of my existence. I bet he offered to come and get the two of us, knowing that he'd likely be interrupting an intimate moment. It's the only way he will ever have the opportunity to use me to get himself off.

Without a word, Rico closes the door on him, turns, then walks back toward me, his dick swinging between his legs, still rock hard. With a smile, he gets under the covers with me. "Where were we?"

Another knock at the door leaves me tempted to grab my gun and put a bullet through it.

"He said now, Rico."

I will be the one to end that guy's life; I promise myself, it will be me.

Cursing under his breath, Rico gets up. He dresses, not saying a word, until he turns to me. I'm still under the duvet, a little wary of his angry, red face. It softens when he looks into my eyes. "I'm sorry, babe, I'm just pissed we don't get to finish what you started." He tries for a smile, but he's still got that look of madness in his eyes.

I didn't realise the extent of the effect my lips have on him.

He holds out his hand for me, lifting me up onto my knees when I take it. Brushing his fingers down my back with whisper softness, he pulls me close to him, my breasts pushing against his warm chest. With his tongue, his licks my top lip, dipping it into my mouth when I open it in response. His kiss is deep, sensual, slow.

When we part, I'm breathless, my eyes closed. I can still feel him on my tingling lips.

"Get dressed, beautiful. This *will be* continued."

It takes me a few seconds to regain my senses. When I'm fully back in my own body, I slide off the bed to get dressed, before we both head downstairs.

The team is already assembled in the lounge, with Dieter pacing the floor in front of the ornate fireplace, everyone's eyes on him. He turns toward us when we enter. "Glad you could join us." He motions with his hand to sit down, his patience wearing thinner as his eyes follow us until we're seated. "In future, fuck on your own time, not mine."

As my face heats – from anger, coupled with mortification – I tell myself that now is probably not the time to remind him that I am back here, hours earlier than he originally asked me to be so, in theory, we were *going* to be fucking on our time, not his. His inadvertence is *our* inconvenience, not the other way around. But, like I said, now is not the time to advise him of that.

Neither one of us says anything.

He doesn't wait for an answer, either. Instead, he picks up a remote control off the table, points it somewhere and clicks. A projector screen unfolds, covering the massive mirror just in front of the fireplace.

If this turns into some boring, high school-type seminar, I'm going to be asleep before the end of it.

Faces flash on the screen, alongside a mini-bio of who each man is – or, more to the point, a list of their crimes, locations, known associates … this is information the agency would cream over.

I know some of the faces I'm seeing; they make me feel sick to my stomach. A lot of the men on screen are known for kidnapping, then selling young girls for cash or drugs – they don't care which, so long as their pockets are lined at the end of it.

Dieter is interested in the latter, of course. He wants to get his hands on their drugs, because he has buyers lined up who would be willing to pay over the odds for the quality of the stuff. Dieter, over the years, has earned himself quite a reputation for being able to deliver exactly what he says he will. So, regardless of what he charges, idiots will flock to him like diseases on rats to get a taste of what he's selling.

This is all well and good, but it leaves me a little empty on the information *I* want. I know Tony wants this guy busted for what he's doing, but he's given me a small window of time to take him down for what *I* know he's doing, and I don't want to miss an opportunity like that. One way or another, he is going to pay for what he's done to me.

Chapter 14

By the time the lecture is over, I'm barely awake. I've been told my role in this – comms. Wonderful; I'm to remain downgraded because Mr. Mob Boss still doesn't trust me, despite Rico's protests. I guess, I knew it would come to this. He did tell me earlier in the day, after all. I'm still not one hundred percent physically fit, either, but that doesn't mean I'm any less pissed.

Rico will be on the front line again.

It's not a massive job, so we're told. It's more about the surveillance this time around, making sure shipments are docked without incident. There will be minimum in the way of muscle at the warehouse, where the deliveries are expected.

I don't know what's in these deliveries, I haven't been privy to that information right now, nor am I likely to be, in order to give Dieter peace of mind. They're not even telling me where they're being delivered, until the very last minute. I've been dismissed from the remainder of the meeting.

Upstairs, I'm sat on the edge of the bed, staring out of the window, watching the luminous moonlight bounce off the waves of the black sea, sparkling with the resplendent glow of the blanket of stars above it. It's beautiful, soothing. The window is open a little, so I can hear the back and forth of the waves in the distance, crashing against one another like a maritime orchestra of countless depths.

The minutes stretch out, sending me stir-crazy as I wait. There's not even anything decent on the flat screen TV. I lie back on the bed, flicking through the channels with the remote, wondering whether I should call Tony, while I have the time. It's probably pointless; I don't have anything to tell him. I know they want me to watch the cameras as a shipment comes in, but I don't know what that shipment contains, I don't know where it's being dropped off, and I don't know when. Wouldn't be much of a call. *Oh, hi, Tony. There's something being delivered soon; I don't know what, I don't know where, and I don't know when, but I thought I'd let you know, OK? Thanks, bye.* A complete waste of my time, and his. I'm hoping I can get some of the details off Rico, whenever he's finished downstairs. Maybe I can sex them out of him.

*

The delectable vibrating of my nerve endings wakes me. My body is flushed, tingling, heated from toe to tip as delicious, melting warmth spreads through my lower limbs.

Eyes rolling, they flicker open. The shadowed room is bathed in the opaline rays of the moon outside, highlighting the gleam in Rico's eyes, as he looks up at me from where he is buried between my thighs, his tongue lapping at my silky lips, pushing deep inside, drawing my juices out to massage into my clit.

I moan a primal sound, tweaking my exposed nipples between thumb and forefinger, as I lift my hips off the bed, rubbing my sodden pussy into his eager lips.

I don't remember nodding off, but what a fucking way to wake up.

"Even in your sleep, you get so wet for me, babe. I couldn't resist."

"Don't let me stop you," I purr, stretching into him, parting my legs further for him.

His tongue flicks out, over and over with expert lashes, pushing against my stimulated clit, causing fresh waves of uninhibited arousal to wash through me.

A pleasured cry escapes my lips when he slides two fingers deep into me. I grip the sheets beneath me with both hands, thrusting up into his touch – desperate for more of whatever he can give me.

The tempo of his movement changes, from one moment to the next. With each assault, my body shudders, my groans alternating between loud, harsh, soft, whispered.

He sucks my trembling bud into his hot mouth.

I hold my breath, feeling the crescendo of my climax bubbling under my prickled skin. Each stroke of my clit catapults me further and further away from my reality; as though I am there, feeling every thrust, every flick, but, at the same time, a feeling of weightlessness overcomes me, like I am drifting away from my body, yet still able to feel every sweet touch.

I scream his name, my body jolting back into existence, arching into him as I explode around his fingers. Still he continues to drive deep into me, urging every last drop of my flooding climax from my weakened body.

I drop back onto the bed – panting, delectably sated – unable to hold my own weight any longer. With a smile, I try to steady my breathing, one hand across my forehead, wiping away the light sheen of perspiration beading my brow.

Rico hoists himself up to lie beside me, raining feathery kisses across my earlobe and down my neck. "I wanna discuss this job Dieter's given us."

It's a way to kill the moment, but it's also music to my ears – just the words I've been longing to hear, since being thrown out of the remainder of this evening's meeting.

He certainly knows how to pick his moments, though. Looking at the bedside clock, I note the early hour. "You wanna do this now? Can't it wait until morning?" My body is heavy, my eyes even more so. I yawn, mostly by accident, but it does serve to help put across my point. "I don't think I can stay awake after that." I nuzzle into him, my head on his chest, listening to the steady beat of his heart.

He doesn't say anything, as he uses his free hand to stroke my hair, after pulling the duvet up and around us both.

I am content, relaxed for the first time in a long time, it seems. The same demons plague me – even now – but I am happy to lose myself to this bliss, for at least a few more hours.

*

Waking, I reach my hand across to Rico's side of the bed, only to find it empty, cold – he's been gone for some time. I look over my shoulder at the clock to see that dawn is fast approaching. I wonder where Rico has gotten to.

The sweet aroma of bacon finds its way to my senses, making my stomach growl. I hope Dieter's still got bagels in.

Swinging my legs off the side of the bed, I stand, stretching out the last of the fatigue wrapped around my bones. I still ache from my wounds, but they're getting better.

I head for the bathroom, locking the door behind me, before I grab my phone down off the light fixture. I have over a dozen text messages, and over three times that amount in missed calls and voicemails. Tony knows I can't constantly be at my phone twenty-four-seven; I'm sure his spies will have followed me to know where I'm staying.

The gist of the messages is about the same – pull my shit together and let him know I'm still breathing, or he'll storm the house, shooting everyone he sees. A tad over dramatic, if you ask me, but then again, he does have a flair for it.

I still don't have much to tell him, so I just let him know that I'm safe, that Dieter has a job lined up, for which I am clueless as to any details. So much for not wasting time telling him precisely fuck all. Last thing I need, though, is for him marching in here thinking he's my knight in shining armor.

Putting my phone back, I have a quick shower. Once dressed, I make my way downstairs, half to find Rico, half following the smell of grilled meat.

The house is pretty much deserted. I find Rico in the kitchen with Dieter, the only other person present is the cook, frying up breakfast over the range.

The two men, sat at the table, lift their heads from their discussion to look at me. Rico smiles, but Dieter remains impassive, his eyes following me when I walk to the fridge for the cream cheese.

I toast and make my own bagel, never having been too comfortable being waited on when I'm quite capable of doing things for myself. It gives me time, too, to decide whether I've got the balls big enough to join the guys at the table, or whether I voice a few pleasantries before making my way back upstairs.

I'm going to have to choose the former – I need to take the opportunity of finding out some intel on the job Dieter's finally allowed me in on.

Putting my breakfast on a plate, I walk over, treading carefully, gauging any obvious signs of animosity that might start pouring from Dieter's body. He doesn't even look at me, even when I take a seat beside Rico.

"Need help with anything?" I'm feeling brave … although, it could actually be desperation; I'll know soon enough.

"No." I'm still not afforded a glance when Dieter barks his single-worded response at me.

OK, time to take my leave. I tried. I failed. I'm leaving, tail between my legs. Picking up my plate, I slide off my chair, heading for the stairs, taking a bite of my breakfast.

"Wait."

I stop in my tracks, the bagel hanging from my mouth as I turn, looking at Dieter, like a man caught with his dick in a chicken. "Hmmm?" I manage, my mouth full.

"Sit."

These one-word non-responses are going to get very tiresome, very quickly. If he wants me to stay, the least he can do is talk to me like a human being, not his pet dog – though, I suspect he actually treats them much better than he does me.

I don't give him the satisfaction of a verbal response – like my own childish version of treating him how he's been treating me – I simply re-take my seat next to Rico and look at Dieter, in anticipation of what he's got to say to me.

"You don't need to know everything, right now, but you will need to know what to look for when the time comes." He turns some photographs toward me, showing me some dark, grainy images of a shipping container. "This is what we're expecting, so it's a little larger than what you're used to, at the moment."

"What's in it?" I fear the answer, enough that I've stopped eating; the sinking, sickening dread bubbling in my stomach.

"You don't need to know that. You just need to know where to look for anyone approaching who shouldn't be there."

"Where's 'there'?"

"You don't need to know that either."

I don't need to know a lot of things, it would seem. I don't understand why he's even dragged me back to the table, when he's given me nothing that I can use. Even *if* I was working for him, this whole conversation is pointless. All it's done, is serve to make me anxious to know what he's transporting in that container, and if it is what I think it might be. If it is, then I need more intel, because Warren will need to know. This could be bigger than anything we've anticipated so far, and would go down a lot better in a court of law, than drug charges.

"So, what exactly do I need to know right now?" There must be a reason he's changed his mind about me being here.

"Study these photographs, make sure you know every single entry and exit point like the back of your hand." He hands me a brown envelope. "There's a list of cameras, and what angle they're pointed at. Memorise them, so that you can call them out the moment you need to. I don't want anything missed, which is why there are two of you on this, not one."

And because you don't trust me to be in the field. There's no need to sugar coat it. I'm a great marksman; I'd be an asset out there, instead of being put to waste watching camera feeds. I know it, he knows it. He's just being a dick.

Chapter 15

Dieter's explained to me what I need to be looking out for, but he still hasn't told me the where or the when. It'll be sprung on me last minute, most likely when everyone's already there, on site, and even then, it might not.

Unbeknownst to him, however, even with the snippet of information and visuals he has given me, I can run it against local areas on our databases, use a process of elimination. The only problem is, I need to get these images over to Warren, somehow, without getting caught. Dieter would question why I'd want to take them with me upstairs – even if I tell him it's to study them, he'll wonder why I need the privacy to do that.

The only alternative is to try and find a way to get my phone downstairs, unseen, undetected, and try to sneak some decent shots that I can store, to send to Warren when I have a better opportunity. The best time for me to do that, I would imagine, is during the dead of night, when there's hardly anyone around. So long as I'm only seen going over the material, I can chalk it up to studying the positionings.

Outside, in the garden, by the pool, I'm on one of the loungers, contemplating the risks of what I need to do. It's hot out, and my choices of black, cut-off jeans and a tank top weren't one of my best. The dark color is eating up the heat, making my skin sizzle beneath the material. It would make sense to head back inside, but, for once, I have solitude out here. There're no barely-dressed bimbos screaming by the pool side, no goons drooling over their tanned skin or fake assets. It's a rare occasion of quiet bliss, which I mean to take advantage of.

My peacefulness is obliterated when I hear the patio doors open, then close, momentarily allowing the multitude of voices indoors, to escape, permeating my tranquillity.

A shadow blocks the sunlight in front of me, making me squint to see who my trespasser is. It's a welcome intrusion when I see Rico smiling down at me. Even more so when he holds up takeout bags, making me understand why he's here – because he's brought food with him.

Hoisting myself up, I move my legs, giving him space to sit beside me as he hands me the bag. I dish out two cheeseburgers, giving him one, then unwrapping my own. The sweet scent of grilled cow, combined with whatever secret sauce they use, makes my stomach rumble.

"Tomorrow is big game for us, babe." Despite having his mouth half-full of meat, Rico gives me just a little bit more of what I need.

So, it's happening tomorrow, which gives me time to get the images across to Warren tonight. More time would have been ideal, but I can still work with this.

My curiosity is peaked. "Big game, how?" Something in my gut is telling me that this is more than the usual drug heists. I don't want to believe it, but I can't shake it. I've never seen Rico get this enthused about a couple of kilos of dope before.

"There's a lot riding on this container, a hell of a lot more than usual."

The more he talks, the sicker I feel. A container of drugs seems like a lot, and not so easy to move as quickly from the docks as something more sinister … like girls. Drugs would take time to load up into several vehicles, a shipment of that size, but girls … girls would only need to be herded into a large truck. No-one cares whether the conditions are so cramped, that it's impossible for any normal human being to breathe. They don't give a shit whether some of them come out of there covered in excrement and other bodily fluids, so long as they clean up well, and fetch a few thousand a piece.

The more Rico continues to talk, eyes-wide, hands animated, the more I want to wring his neck. He *can't* be involved like this; he just can't. Dieter must be holding something over him – maybe it's because of my fuck ups, maybe he's making Rico pay for my mistakes. So many maybes, not enough answers. And throughout it all, all I can see is the dead, snow-white faces of the young girls we've found dumped in alleyways. The ones who were little over fifteen years old; their short lives cruelly stolen away from them because they had the misfortune of being pretty, the dreams of coming to Miami to soak up the sun, bag themselves a rich guy to take care of them, begin the success of a modelling career – whichever fucking cliché you choose to go with.

At the end of the day, it doesn't matter when we find them dead in a ditch, glassy eyed and frothing at the mouth from an overdose. They don't ask for a life of pleasuring old, fat, greasy men. They don't beg to be laced with narcotics in order to get through each terrifying, sweaty ordeal.

And they don't ask to be tortured to death for refusing to succumb to the disgusting, sexual desires of the evil men who buy them.

Just like my sister.

I can't. I can't do this right now.

If Rico notices the hot tears welling in the corners of my eyes, I'm as good as dead. I can't afford for this to go tits up; I need to put my game face back on.

Faking a couple of sneezes, I wipe away the tears threatening to fall and laugh it off; voicing my concerns over not coming down sick at a time like this, lest my watery vision get the better of me when I'm focusing on the cameras.

Whether Rico believes me or not, I don't know. He continues to give away only the smallest of details about the job while we eat.

I force the rest of my burger down me. I feel so nauseous that I've lost my appetite. Each piece of meat that slides down my throat threatens to reappear in a torrent of projectile vomit which each photograph I recall seeing, each face, each crime scene; each one a fatal victim of their own hopes and dreams.

The only way I am able to keep from snapping the metal of the lounger legs off, and shoving it through his jugular, is because those inner voices of mine – the ones that urge me to seek my revenge – are reminding me that this is what I've been working so hard for.

That, and because I still cannot accept that Rico is fully in the know about what he's doing. But, the more he talks, the more I am unsure. It turns my body ice cold, because the realisation has dawned on me.

I am in love with Rico. I am in love with a man who could turn out to be a cold-hearted, sociopathic killer, who gets off on selling girls for sex.

*

I can't settle. I haven't been able to let Rico touch me since this afternoon. Lying in bed next to him, looking at his sleeping form, I have a headache from trying to analyse everything I know or have discovered about the man since my coming here. He's always talked about the drugs, never the girls, always the drugs. The jobs we've worked together, or the ones he did during my initiation, have never been about trafficking. That's always been Dieter's bag, to the best of my knowledge. Dieter and Sirus are the ones who are heavily involved with that side of the business.

Dieter has many men – and some women – who work for him. He has always used their strengths to his advantage. If he's managed to encourage those in the sex trade game away from his competitors, then he's kept them in that line of work.

Rico has always been involved with the drug trade. His previous boss – Dieter's deceased brother – used his connections to line his pockets from other dealers. Rico was big on the club scene, selling pills to party-goers. After Dieter slaughtered his own brother, he employed Rico for bigger, better things in that same trade.

I did my research on this. I did extensive studies on each of Dieter's men, finding nothing that would suggest Rico's involvement in trafficking.

Perhaps Dieter is promoting from within the ranks, this time.

I can't let that happen.

Who are you kidding? Are you hoping to lure Rico away from a life of crime? Do you think he's going to give up what he has purely for you? I never thought far enough ahead as to what it would mean for Rico and me after all this is over. It's what he knows; it's not like Dieter is his enemy. Once he's behind bars, or dead, am I expecting Rico to run off into the sunset with me? Do I even want him to, now?

Rico is a criminal – where do I honestly think this is gonna go once my job is done? He'll hate me; likely hunt me down and kill me for the insult. And, damn it, the thought sends a stab of pain lancing through my chest. Hot tears sting my eyes, and I wipe them away with a quick flick of my fingers.

I've got myself buried deep in one fine, fucked up mess. I need to regain my focus. Contrary to what Warren believes, my aim has always been to make Dieter pay for what he did to my sister two years ago. My family and I need closure. We were never given the opportunity of burying her, but have come to terms with the fact that she's likely dead. Or, rather, they have. I've never given up hope.

The list – the one I needed from Bruno – contained the names of the girls that went missing at the same time as my sister. It would've told me their whereabouts, so that I could have at least questioned them, found out if they knew her, where she might have gone, what might have happened to her.

That's gone, now. All that's left is to get that information from the horse's mouth. I am going to torture Dieter to within an inch of his life, until he gives up what happened to my sister. I need my own, personal closure. It's the only reason I still walk this earth.

Making sure Rico is still sound asleep, I creep out of bed as quiet as I can, heading for the bathroom to retrieve my phone. I put on a cardigan, slipping the phone up one of the long sleeves, before making my way downstairs.

It's silent as the grave as I head for the kitchen, where Dieter has left the envelope of images I need for Warren. Lifting one of the dining chairs off the floor – to avoid it scraping on the tiles – I sit down, emptying the contents of the envelope onto the table.

I take my phone out, snapping away at what I need. I'll send them later, at the moment, my ass is twitching from the anticipation that I might get caught. My hands are shaking, sweating, making holding the phone increasingly difficult.

"What are you doing?"

I drop the phone in fright, balking at the loud thump it makes on the thick wood. My head snaps up to see Sirus, stood in the doorway. "Nothing." I try, but I can't keep the quiver out of my voice.

“Doesn’t look like nothing.” He stalks closer, his eyes on my phone.

I grab for it, standing. It doesn’t matter what excuse I try to fob him off with, he’s not going to buy a single one of them. The evil intent in his slit-eyed glare tells me at least that, as I back up, into the sideboard.

“Hand it over.” He holds his palm out, but he’s stupid if he thinks I’m going to make it that easy for him.

I shake my head. “Hell no.” With my free hand, I fumble around on the work surface behind me, desperately seeking something I can use to defend myself. “You want it, you come and take it from me.” Brave words for one not armed.

Especially so, as Sirus pulls out a flick knife from his pocket. “With pleasure,” he sneers, advancing further.

I might have been stupid enough to have goaded a man with a blade into battling with me for possession of my phone, but I’m thankful he hasn’t got the sense enough to yell out, alerting everyone in the household as to what I’ve been doing. Maybe he thinks he can have his way with me first, before he guts me with his knife. He's not going to want interruptions for that.

Before I can find anything behind me, Sirus is on me, blade to my throat as he painfully palms my breasts with his rough hands, moving them down, cupping my genitals with just as much force.

I close my eyes against the ache he leaves behind.

"I've waited for a moment like this since I first laid eyes on you." He licks the side of my face, making me heave.

"Funny," I retort, "since I first laid eyes on you, I've felt constantly sick."

He slaps me, leaving my cheek stinging with hot pain. Grabbing me around the throat with his free hand, he hisses at me, "Bitch." The cold steel of his knife still rests against the flesh of my neck, the tip digging in as his anger grows more palpable. "Question now is, do I fuck you dead, or alive?"

I spit in his face. “I’d probably get more pleasure out of it, if I were dead. It’s the only way your flaccid dick is getting anywhere near me.”

“We’ll see about that.” He removes the knife from my neck, using it, instead, to cut into the flimsy material of my underwear.

I seize the opportunity before he gets his chance. Headbutting him, I push him away from me during his momentary state of disorientation.

He stumbles into the dining table, making much more noise than I care for. I need to shut him up, or he’s going to scream at the top of his lungs, letting everyone know what’s going on. I’ll be dead for sure then.

Holding his forehead in one hand, the other – the one with the knife – aimlessly flaps around.

I snatch the blade from his hand, with my right; with my left hand, I hold the back of his sweaty neck, then force the sharp tip upwards, into his throat, once, twice, three times.

Thick fluid coats my hands, drips to the floor in bulbous globules. I take the weight of the dead man as he slumps forward, easing him to the floor.

Standing, chest heaving, body shaking, I survey the damage I've caused. How the hell am I going to get rid of his body before people start to wake up? Assuming no one heard the noise, of course.

I can't hear any commotion from any other part of the house. Perhaps it just seemed loud to me, considering the intense circumstances. Isn't that how it usually works?

I stay, standing, for long moments, waiting to hear footsteps, voices, anything to suggest that people are awake, but I hear nothing. I can breathe easy. In reality, I probably still have a couple of hours before anyone else is awake. It's nowhere near time enough to figure out where I'm going to dump Sirus's body, but I need to start thinking.

I can't move too freely around the house; I'm covered in blood, blood I could do without traipsing everywhere, making it harder to ensure I cover my tracks.

Come on, Evie, think. This is what you do; it's what you're good at.

Looking around the kitchen, I spot a few cleaning products. They'll come in handy for afterwards.

Heading for the sink, I clean my hands and arms. I've got a small cut on my finger, where the blade slipped, but I should be able to hide it easily enough. I doubt Dieter's going to run his own police investigation as thoroughly as I would, so I won't worry about it right now.

Once done, I head for the patio doors. Opening them, I allow myself to be cooled by the breeze rushing in for a few seconds longer than I should.

The pool is covered with tarpaulin, which I pull off. It's a sizeable sheet, but it's all I can think to use. Lining the doorway with it, I drag what's left over to Sirus's body, rolling him onto it. It takes all my strength to, then, drag him outside, careful not to smear any blood on the tiled floor – the less I have to clean, the better; there's already a puddle of it on the marble.

I reach the poolside, use the tarpaulin to wrap up Sirus, then try, as carefully as I can, to take most of his bulk as I lower him into the water. I can't afford for him to make a splash as his body hits.

With success, I watch him merge underwater, his blood swirling like dark ink around the immediate area. Come morning, it will have tainted a vast majority of the pool. Someone will see it, as Sirus is using the cover as a death shroud. Dieter will hit the roof, want to see all of his men at once. The question now poses itself – how can I make it look as though someone else did it?

I go back into the house, eager to get started on cleaning up.

It takes some time, but I'm happy that I have removed all traces of a struggle from the kitchen. I still have Sirus's knife, which I intend to use in an attempt to implicate another member of the household. That's going to be the tricky part. With only a limited amount of time left until dawn, I will need to tread very carefully.

Chapter 16

Shudders run through the length of me, a dampness pools beneath me, soaking my panties. When my eyes flicker open, I spy Rico above me, his tongue flicking the very tip of my nipple.

I want to turn away … I think. I should turn away; he might be a monster. He might be turning into a monster. I might be able to save him. Either way, my body is connected to his, I can't tear myself from under him – I don't even try.

A war rages inside me, but I am powerless to choose a side.

A groan escapes my lips – whether from pleasure, or anxious turmoil, I can't be sure.

Rico looks up at me, the corners of his dark eyes creased with the sinful smile on his lips. Eyes still on mine, he dips back down, taking my nipple between his lips, sucking, biting.

My body betrays me, arches deeper into him, begs for more without me having to open my mouth. I am treading a dangerously, thin line; one that compromises my morals, my judgement, my integrity, but I cannot seem to bring myself back to the right side of it.

His touch is poison, and the more I get from him, the more I become immune to its devastating effects; the more I want.

He slides his body up against mine, the head of his hard dick teasing my wet folds, dipping into the entrance with only the slightest penetration.

"More," I cry, my voice a quivering shambles. "I want all of you."

He doesn't give me what I want, he prolongs my sensual torment, easing inside me, then out again before that delicious pop.

I love it, but it drives me crazy all at the same time.

He grabs my throat. Not so hard that I can't breathe, but hard enough to cause concern.

I know Rico can get a little rough, but he's never grabbed me like this before. It's not unpleasant, but it's different.

Grip tightening, he slams into me.

Pain erupts, quickly replaced by immense pleasure when he pulls out, slow, purposeful. In he drives again; each thrust hard, deep, yet each time he draws out, the friction against my tight walls sends me into a tailspin.

My body is beautifully beaten by his onslaught, taken higher with each solid stroke. I barely register the hand around my throat, it's almost like its heightening my pleasure threshold.

He draws all the way out, then paws at me, turning me onto my stomach.

Lifting my ass up a little, I give him access to the wet delights between my legs.

He grabs hold of my hips, then pushes into me. He is so hard, and I am so tight in this position, that I can feel every ridge of his cock rubbing me from the inside out. I feel the swell pulsate against my walls, turning my legs to jelly. His large, full balls bounce off my sodden sex, sending electrified tingles through my stomach, down my legs.

His ferocity builds, so much so, that the headboard pounds the wall behind it, the noise drowned out only by my carnal cries of exquisite decadence.

With one, strong hand, he grabs my long hair, twisting it around his fist.

I'm pulled backwards, the faster and harder he fucks me. I can feel some of my hair being ripped from the roots. His animalistic behavior both scares and excites me.

A scream echoes through the house, only it isn't mine.

Whoever it belongs to, Rico ignores it. He is somewhere else, somewhere dark, deep … and that's not a euphemism.

As I twist my body to try and see his face, to somehow make him register the sounds downstairs, he isn't even looking at me. It's as though he's staring off into space, in a whole other world, somewhere even I don't think I am with him.

"Rico." I try to pull away from him, but his strong hands keep me in place. I call his name again, telling him to stop, that he's beginning to hurt me.

His grip on my hair tightens, forcing my gaze away from him.

I kick out with my back leg, catching him in his thigh.

"Shit," he gasps.

Scrambling up the bed, I throw the duvet around me, turning to face whatever he's become. "What the hell?"

His eyes are vacant, staring through me, rather than at me.

"Rico, where were you?" Because he sure as hell isn't here, with me.

Another scream cuts through some of the tension.

Rico shakes his head, trying to instil some sensibility back into himself, before he jumps off the bed, dresses, then heads out of the room, urging me to follow.

I'm not sure I can. I think, largely, because I know why someone is screaming, but also, because my legs are fucked, and not necessarily in a good way. My whole body is shivering, though it's warm in the room; I can't feel any heat in any of my extremities.

I know I will have to go down, though, otherwise Dieter will suspect me right away.

Sitting on the bed, I dress as quick as I can, then make my way to the stairs, holding onto the bannister for dear life, in case my legs give out.

Sure enough, there's a small gathering in the kitchen, just in front of the patio doors. One of the bimbos, her face pale, stained with tears, is being comforted by another at the kitchen table. She looks ready to puke; they both do.

Dieter hasn't made his way down, yet, but it won't be long.

Rico comes in from outside, his head bowed. He's followed closely by one of the twins – Frankie. He's still got the smudge of blood on his forehead that I planted during the early hours.

Frankie is my safest bet to pin this on – when he sleeps, even a rock concert right next to his ear wouldn't wake him. He always takes something before he goes to bed, otherwise he'll stay up all night, off his tits on drink and drugs.

Rico sits him at the table with the girls, then pulls a gun on him, telling him not to move until Dieter's dealt with him. He sends another of the goons to rifle through Frankie's belongings upstairs.

Dieter passes the lackey in the kitchen doorway, a look of terrifying thunder on his reddening face. His jaw is tight, pulsing with barely-contained rage. "Would someone like to explain what the fuck is going on?" I imagine he's seen some of carnage outside – his bedroom window overlooks the gardens; he's probably looked outside before coming downstairs.

Rico tries to explain to him that Sirus is dead – the cause unknown. “Frankie’s got blood on him. I’ve sent Dan upstairs to check out his room.”

Dieter flashes me a quick look, but I can’t decipher his thoughts fast enough. Didn’t look good, in any case. “What happened to you?” His focus is back on me, his gaze trained on my neck.

I look down, not able to see too much, given that my head is attached to my neck – for now. And then I understand. I look at Rico, who’s looking back at me.

“Don’t tell me.” Dieter heads outside, content, for the time being, that the red marks that must be around my neck, are not there as a result of whatever he’s walking into.

When he comes back in, his gun is in his hand. He stomps right over to Frankie, levelling the gun against his temple. “You had better hope they find nothing upstairs.”

Frankie is white, trembling from head to toe. “It wasn’t me, boss, I would never do that to Sirus. I would never do that to *you.* You guys are my family.” He sounds desperate, but I don’t doubt that there’s truth to what he’s saying. To all others, I’m hoping it sounds like he’s clinging.

Dan comes downstairs, his straight face solemn. He nods once, then holds out his hand. In his palm is Sirus's flick knife, covered in his blood. "Found it stashed in his dresser." Exactly where I put it. "It was wrapped up in a t-shirt."

"No way, man, no way." Frankie tries to stand, but Dieter forces him back down with a hand on his shoulder. "No fuckin' way, I didn't do it, that's been planted. Boss, I didn't do it." He turns to Dieter, his eyes wide, watery.

I should feel some remorse, but I can't bring myself to. Frankie, like his brother, and every other goon in this house, is scum. I've set out to see them all fall, and I done caring by what means.

Dieter looks up at me. "Kill him," he says, handing me the gun.

What? Is this a test? If I shoot him, will he forgive and forget, let me back in? I don't see any other way out of this. If I do it, I'm a murderer, a killer of my own making in a way. If I don't do it, Dieter will, then he will likely do the same to me.

Moving to stand behind Frankie, I place the gun at the back of his head. He's pleading for his life, crying, his words muffled by the amount of saliva that's accumulated between his lips.

I fire.

He drops on the table, his face smeared in his own blood and brain matter. The wound on his head open, raw, jagged skin surrounding the coagulated, red mess of tissue and bone.

I hand the gun back to Dieter, then walk away.

*

I've come back to the hotel, desperate to get away from the nightmare that is Dieter's house. With two dead bodies – both of my doing – contaminating the air there, I needed some breathing space. I told Rico I wanted to be alone for a couple of hours, but that I would be back for the briefing for tonight's job.

It's going ahead, thankfully. Dieter isn't going to let two deaths deter him from what he wants. Sirus might have been a key player in tonight's mission, but Frankie won't be sorely missed. He's already replaced them both. Unfortunately, not with me, so I will still be babysitting them all on camera, hoping that Warren will be able to work out where they are before the container gets transported elsewhere.

Booting up my laptop, I sit at my desk, waiting for the screen to load. In the meantime, I hook my phone up to the computer, ready to send over the images. I don't have the time to text them and wait for a response, I need to do this now, live, and as quickly as possible.

Once I'm up and running, I open a secure link on my video call app, hit Warren's name, then wait.

A small screen pops up with my image. I grimace at my haggard appearance, noting the dark smudges under my eyes. In comparison, Tony's bearded, handsome face fills the remainder of my screen.

"You're looking good, Evie. Miami air agrees with you."

He must be joking, I look like the living dead, and I don't feel much better, either. "Pull the other one. I have something for you, and I need something back, like three hours ago."

"What you got?"

I send over the images of the docks, the warehouse, the cameras, as well as telling Warren what little information I have. "I think it's girls, Tony. There's no way a container this large is full of drugs. It would take too much time, and too much manpower to shift it all before sunrise."

Warren contemplates what I've said, his eyes darting from right to left, taking in the imagery. "You need to step away from this, Evie, this is not what we came for."

I sit upright. "Are you fucking kidding me? This is bigger than what we came for; this is what you gave me time to uncover. I'm not stepping down from this; I will find out where that location is, and I will save those girls from the life they'll likely end up with."

Warren knows how my sister's disappearance has affected me from day one. Once upon a time, we were lovers, but after what happened, I pushed him away. I couldn't give my love to someone, when I struggled to even love myself after losing such a large part of me.

Besides, the life we lead is a dangerous, unpredictable one. Sometimes we're forced to fuck drug lords, or their wingmen, in order to get what we want. I wouldn't wish that on anyone I claimed to love. The many possible outcomes of such scenarios, I would wish on them even less.

"You can't do this on your own."

"The hell I can't." I've had a death wish ever since my sister's kidnap. I took this job on, knowing that the actuality of me dying would be high. I didn't care then, and I don't care now. "If you wanna help, you need to find me this location."

"You need to learn to take your orders seriously." His tone has lowered, taken on a hint of anger. "I am your damn boss, and I am telling you to stand down on this until we can get you the manpower you need. One against an unknown number is certain death."

I know, but it won't stop me.

Chapter 17

I told Warren to do what he could, to find me a location. He knows I can't go in there, guns blazing, until he gives me that information, so I don't know why he's being so overdramatic. He won't even tell me until he's standing on the doorstep, just to be sure I won't run in like a one-man army.

I'm leaving my departure to the last minute. I've packed up all my belongings, ready to make a clean, hasty getaway at the first opportunity. After tonight, I'm praying that I have enough to take Dieter down.

My taxi arrives, alerting me via text message. I stash my phone in my underwear, then grab the bag I need for tonight, leaving the others behind.

The drive back to Dieter's is a stifling one; I spend the majority of it with the window rolled down, gulping back as much fresh air as I can. Doesn't seem to have made any difference as we pull into Dieter's driveway; I still feel as sick as dog.

I pay the cabbie, grab my bag, then get out.

Back indoors, voices filter through the foyer from the lounge. Bag over my shoulder, I head in that direction. I push open the door to find the team assembled around the coffee table, chatting, discussing plans, drinking. Great idea to be consuming alcohol before a job, but this isn't my party, so I don't comment. I'm hoping it might dull the wits of some them enough, that one of them might slip me a location without much aggressive persuasion on my part.

"Welcome back, baby." Rico takes my bag off me, kissing me on the cheek. "Come join us, we're just going over what's going to happen tonight."

As I listen to them talk, I understand that we're going to be pulling this off during the shift of a team of workmen, who're also moving containers into the yard adjacent. They're doing legitimate work, whereas this lot are going to try and blend in, make out that they're doing the same.

An HGV will be waiting to take the container to a secured part of the yard, where we will have armed men stationed, waiting to take delivery. It'll stay there for forty-eight hours, before the next shift of workmen come in to move, then it, too, will be taken to an undisclosed location, where a bidding war will start.

There's no way this is drugs. Dieter doesn't have auctions on his dope, he's has buyers lined up before he even has the drugs in his possession. Stupid, some might say, but then others know not to fuck with him.

Regardless, the fact that there's going to be a bidding war, tells me it's girls. It must be. Part of me wants nothing to do with this; I don't want to be responsible for bringing innocent youngsters into a life of debauchery, if I don't manage to pull this off. On the other hand, I've little choice. I *need* this. I need to see the look of shock and fear on Dieter's face as I take him down, once and for all.

Not one of these bastards has divulged the location to me, yet, so I might need to get physical when the numbers are whittled down.

Dieter's going to be on the front line, with Rico and others, which convinces me all the more that it's girls. If it were drugs, Dieter would be right here, not giving a fuck, but the trafficking of innocents pays the majority of his bills, so he has always overseen this side of things.

A sickness dizzies my brain. Rico must know what's happening tonight, there's no way he couldn't. Dieter would have told him. Why is he doing it? Does he have his way with any of them? Does he torture them? Does he strip them down and help parade them in front of their vile audience?

Perhaps he will just play a small part. Perhaps he can't say no, because Dieter will kill him. Perhaps, perhaps, perhaps, maybe, maybe, maybe. This is all too much; it must end here. Those girls must not leave that dock in two days' time. I *will* find them. I *will* save them all.

It's not long before the team are kitting up and moving out. I'm left alone with Lucas, Dan and Harris. Harris is stupidly drunk, struggling to string together a coherent sentence as he cries over the death of his brother.

It's not ideal, leaving him here with me, considering I'm the one that put a bullet in Frankie, but since he can't stand unaided, I'm not too concerned that he'll be able to extract any sort of revenge for it.

Lucas is instructing me on which cameras I will be looking at, and which ones he will. It's simple enough; I'm pretty sure I can't fuck it up.

As the first of the goons come into sight, we ready ourselves to switch between feeds, making sure they haven't been followed, and aren't getting any suspicious looks from the hard-working non-criminals also on the yard.

The red, metal container is on a large ship, docking already. The sight makes me edgy as hell, I'm fidgeting in my seat, trying to keep my shit together before Lucas decides I'm useless and slits my throat.

Swapping camera angles, I take as many opportunities as I can to try and work out where the location is. I haven't had time to check my phone, to see if Warren has found anything out. I might need to fake a toilet break soon, to see if he has anything for me. I check my watch six or seven times in as many minutes, wondering why it's taking so long to get the container off the boat.

"You got some place you need to be?" Stands to reason Lucas would notice my restlessness.

"I need the bathroom," I lie, bouncing up and down in the chair. "I'm waiting for the right moment; I don't wanna miss something on screen that might jeopardise this job. I can't afford for any more hiccups." I throw him a nervous smile, hoping he buys my story.

"Go now," he tells me, "I'll need you more focused for the next part."

Score! I jump up from my chair, racing out of the room.

Once locked in the bathroom, I fish my phone out, checking for updates. Nothing. Absolutely fuck all. Warren knows the importance of this; if I find he's holding out on me, I will be pissed beyond words. If I fail tonight because of it, I will make sure he suffers every bit as much as I know I will. They can't get away with this.

Quick as I can, I fire off a text message, letting him know that the container – wherever its location – will be there for no more than forty-eight hours. If we don't find it before then, those girls are as good as dead, and I will slaughter Dieter myself, legitimately or otherwise.

I hide my phone, then make my way back to the lounge. Lucas tells me I'm back just in time – the container is off the boat, ready to be transported to the main yard. Retaking my seat, I don my headset, and focus on the screens, giving instructions when and where needed.

It feels wrong, helping these men direct that metal prison to somewhere more secure, somewhere where they can open it to check on their *goods*, scare them even more, torture them, taunt them, get off on the look of pure terror etched into each of their dirt-strewn faces.

A crackling interrupts my thoughts.

"Assistance required at two, two, nine, nine Port Boulevard, multiple ten-thirty-eights, proceed with caution."

Turning my head, I spot a police scanner over the fireplace. I wrack my brain, *ten-thirty eights ... suspicious individuals*. Port Boulevard is … *oh, fuck.*

Agony shoots through my head. It disorientates me, but doesn't knock me out. I throw my arm up to block the second smack to the temple from Lucas's gun butt. I hurl out a punch with my free hand, smashing it against Lucas's face, hearing his nose crack.

He falls back into the chair, blood gushing from the broken appendage, his eyes rolling.

I seize his gun, whacking him over the head with it. Aiming it at him, my finger hovers over the trigger.

I'm hurtled to the side, rolling around on the floor with a drunken Harris, whose senses seem to have returned enough to launch a flimsy attack.

He shouldn't have bothered, though. The alcohol has battered his brain, causing him to swerve unsteadily as he tries to straddle me. He can't even see straight; his eyes are struggling to gain focus on me.

The gun has fallen from my grasp, but it doesn't discourage me. With both hands free, I throw punch after punch at Harris's face, until he drops to the side with a loud grunt.

Finding the gun, I launch myself at it, landing on my side as I make a grab for it.

Lucas has come to, is stomping toward me, his face a disastrous sight.

Swinging my arm around, I aim for him, squeezing the trigger twice. One bullet catches him in the chest, the other his jaw, both in quick succession before his body even has chance to thud to the floor.

I clamber to my feet, gun still in hand, eyes on Harris as he writhes on the floor like a turtle on its back.

I shoot him in the face.

Dark splashes of blood spray the fireplace, as well as the rug beneath him. He's not getting up now for shit, dozy fucker.

Holstering the gun in my pants, I check the cameras. The container has been moved to its location – the yard at South Florida Container Terminal … two, two, nine, nine Port Boulevard. It's closer to me than any other unit who might be responding to that call out. I'm right on top of it. If I look out of the window, I can see the twinkling of the lights illuminating the yard.

Grabbing Lucas's car keys, I head outside, tapping at the alarm button to determine which vehicle is his.

The lights flash on a brand-new Porsche. *Perfect*. This will get me there in no time at all.

I climb inside, start the engine, then wheel spin off the property, swerving slightly before I get a handle on the damn thing.

Chapter 18

As close as I am, the journey takes a lot longer than I want it to.

The police scanner only reported suspicious characters. As of yet, there has been no gunfire, or anything else to warrant an immediate, urgent response. I'm hoping that Dieter doesn't have any kind of scanner on him, either, otherwise he would have heard the transmission, and be looking to make alternative arrangements.

Heading down North Cruise Boulevard, I'm a stones throw away from my destination. I dump the car near the Norwegian Cruise Line, then run the rest of the way.

It's not difficult to duck and dive my way out of the spotlight – the Terminal closed hours ago, so there isn't much in the way of security. It's probably why Dieter chose it, but it might be swarming at some point, once the local police get wind of what's going on here.

Before I left the villa, I checked on the location of the container, as well as, roughly, how many goons I would be facing. If I can take out one of the shooters hidden away, then I can use his sniper rifle to get rid of the other two, who I know are lurking somewhere in the shadows.

Keeping close to the corrugated offices, I head toward the yard I need. I know one of the shooters is on the roof of an office, somewhere along this line. He's going to be trained on the container, rather than watching his back.

Dieter might have wanted to keep me in the dark regarding this job, but telling me details such as positions and lookouts, will be his undoing. The information will be more useful than he could have imagined, given my training.

Spying some rungs on the side of one of the offices, I make my silent way up, slowing when I near the top. Peering over the edge, I can see one of Dieter's goons in position, on his stomach, sights trained somewhere in front of him.

With soundless movements, I haul myself fully onto the roof, staying low, the shadows concealing my presence. The gun in my hand isn't silenced, like I suspect his weapons are, but I see the handle of a blade sticking out of a pouch on his belt.

If I'd had more time, I would have better armed myself, but if the police got here before Warren, then there'd have been a devastating shoot out, with much of the local law enforcement losing their lives, given the level of organisation on Dieter's part. I couldn't risk that, so I will have to make do with what's in front of me.

The goon loses momentary focus, as he scratches his nose. I launch myself over his body, covering his mouth with one hand as I grab for the knife with the other. Pulling it from his pouch, I pull his head back, then slide the cold metal across the exposed flesh of his throat. It flaps open, oozing thick blood down his neck.

He gurgles, trying to shout out, but it's useless.

When he stops moving, I search him for weapons, grabbing a Sig, the silenced rifle and another blade. Once done, I roll him off the building, into the darkness, where he should lie, undiscovered, until this is over.

Lying to the right of his blood pool, I peer down the rifle's sight, searching for the other two, who I know are close.

There's a water tower opposite me, perfect for a lookout. I adjust the lens on my scope, bringing it into focus on a man, dressed in all black – one of Dieter's. He's looking away from me, somewhere toward the main entrance.

I'm a little disappointed that he won't know it's me that killed him, as my fired bullet sails through the air to strike him in the head. His black blood decorates the tower beside him as he falls, out of sight behind the railings.

One more; I know there's another sniper somewhere.

Try as I might, I can't find his position. Time is running out, I need to get to Dieter before the police arrive.

Moving from my position, I gather my arsenal, then head down the side of the building, jumping over the body of the dead goon.

I make sure to stay in the shadows, keeping one eye trained on my surroundings, in case the other sniper makes a surprise appearance. Not to mention the other lackeys that might be roaming.

I jog, quickly, but quietly around the buildings and containers, to see that a crane is still moving the one I want. Beneath it, several of Dieter's men are directing the driver on where to drop it.

There's a small warehouse some feet away, with lights on inside. My best guess is that Dieter is in there. Whether he is alone, though, is another matter entirely.

Ducking behind some metal oil drums, I watch what the group of men do. One says something to another, then branches off, jogging casually behind one of the containers.

I follow him, to find that he's taking a leak. His back is to me, he's unaware of my presence. I creep up, just as he is zipping up his pants, then I grab his neck with my arm, twisting until it snaps.

I drop his body to the floor, then take his gun.

From my position, I am closer to the warehouse. The other goons are facing the opposite direction. If I'm quick, I could make it inside without them being any the wiser.

I take one step forward, before a bullet whizzes passed my face.

Shit! I've been made. The other sniper must have seen me. Any moment now, he will be alerting the men as to my location. *Think fast, Evie.*

Retracing my steps, I duck behind the small office, listening for voices, footsteps. I can hear garbled Russian, one telling another in which direction I ran.

This is going tits up. Dieter will know, by now, that I am here. That's if his cronies have recognised my face. I might still have luck on my side, my identity still a mystery to them. However, I'm going to work on the assumption that they know it's me.

Footsteps, though slower, are creeping closer. They're being cautious, wondering where I might spring from. I can use this to my advantage. Grasping the ladder to my left, I hurry back onto the roof of the sniper building. From the shadows, I lean over the edge, the Sig trained below, hovering over the dead goon.

Two figures come into my line of sight. As hoped, they are momentarily distracted by their deceased friend. Shock mars their faces as they look at one another. The one furthest from me catches sight of me from the corner of his eye. He opens his mouth to say something, but chews on my bullet instead. Before the other can register, he's got my next shot embedded in his skull.

I can still hear raised voices all around me, and there's still the matter of the hidden sniper.

If memory serves, the bullet that almost hit me came from a good height, from my right-hand side. Perhaps not as high as the water tower, but still something a good distance off the ground. It's obvious, now, that he's got his eye on the warehouse. Makes sense, if Dieter is in there, that he'd be protecting his boss.

He needs to go. If I can get rid of him, I can still slip by the rest of them, into the building. I can take care of Dieter just as back up arrives to finish off those outside. I hope.

Staying under cover of darkness, I look for opportune locations close to the warehouse. Where would I position myself out here?

Of course, the gantry. It's the perfect spot.

I refocus my attention on its framework, ascending, scoping out any obvious hiding spots. It's a quick flash from something reflective that gives him away. Maybe the same can be said of me, as he is training his sight directly on me.

I fire two shots. The first distracts him, as I hoped it would. The second, as I moved a touch to the left, anticipating a small movement of his head, penetrates between his eyes, bursting from the back of his skull amid a glittering display of reds and whites.

Job done, I climb back down the building, shouldering the rifle, drawing the Sig instead.

The voices are further away, so I head back in the direction of the warehouse, praying that I get the opportunity to slip inside, unseen. Against the corrugated steel of the outer walls, I wait, looking out for any of Dieter's men.

When no-one appears, I slide through the half open door, using the racking inside for cover. I can hear only one voice, coming from the middle of the open space.

Dieter is on the phone, his angered face rigid, contorted. He runs a hand through his messy hair. "This wasn't supposed to fucking happen," he spits. "Get the car here, now." He ends the call, looking to throw the phone at the wall, but rethinks his decision, instead, gripping it until his knuckles turn white.

I level the gun at him. "Turn around. Slowly."

He does as instructed.

I'm perplexed to see a sly smile stretched across his features. It unnerves me, in the same way that much of his persona does. "What have you got to be happy about, *boss?*"

"Oh, Evie," he trills, "I have much to be happy about."

He's called me by my real name … but how does he know? No-one knows. Or so I thought. My brow creases, my breath hitches. "Evie?" I stammer.

"Evelyn Baker." His saccharine grin widens. "The look on your face is priceless. I imagine you'd hoped to see a similar look on mine, as you strutted in here, completely unaware that you've been taken for a ride." He chuckles to himself. "And, this time, not in a good way."

"What do you mean?" I hate that I have to give him the satisfaction of my bewilderment by asking, but I need to know what he means. Lives depend on it.

"That container outside is empty."

What?! Why? What is the point of that? I'm baffled beyond comprehension. "You've lost me." Even trying to keep my cool, keep my words from stammering all over the place is a difficult feat. "Why would you be shipping an empty container?"

He takes a seat, so blasé, confident, smug. "That was for your benefit, Princess. As soon as I learned who you are – I knew I should never have trusted you. I wanted to lure you here on purpose."

"To what end?" He has my interest piqued, much to my chagrin. Who's been telling him about me? Who knows about me? I've been so careful.

"My shipment came in yesterday. They're already gone from here." I hate that Dieter looks so pleased with himself. I feel like a fool. "The girls had an extra addition to keep them company, someone you know, someone who, up until your arrival, had the same position, in the same bed that you have now."

I'm going to be sick. The implications of what he's saying make my stomach churn. He can't possibly mean what I think he does. He can't. Rico wouldn't. Would he? A chill runs up and down my spine, deadening my legs, liquifying my brain as I try to process his insinuations.

"You're lying." Tears sting the corners of my eyes. I try to hold them in, desperate for him not see me crumble, but so much is making sense. I don't want it to, I almost reject it as bullshit, but I can't deny the smells, the emotions, everything I picked up on in that room that I brushed aside, things I couldn't place at the time.

I squeeze the trigger the moment the tears fall.

The power of the bullet launches him backwards. Crimson stains spread across his chest, discoloring the white of his shirt as he crashes to the concrete.

"You look like her, you know?"

His voice sends shivers through my entire body, for completely different reasons than they used to. I turn to face Rico, tears still falling freely. "Why?"

He snorts. "That's a contradicting question, coming from you." He steps closer to me. "You tried to deceive us, get accepted, get intel, then have us locked up, and *you're* asking *me* why I've turned the tables?"

Pure hate courses through me. My previous feelings for him are momentarily interrupted by seething anger. "Are you fucking kidding me? You're a dirty, low-life criminal out to line his pockets at the expense, and the deaths, of others. Do not compare what I have done to anything you've managed to pull off. I am *nothing* like you."

"Oh, but Evie, you are."

It dawns on me, then, as he says my name in that sugary tone, that I've heard it come from his lips once before. On the beach, as he made love to me. *You feel so good, Evie. I love the way you make me feel.*

My stomach turns.

"You murdered your way into this gang, or had you forgotten? Your hands are stained with blood, too."

"That blood does not belong to innocent people." I clench my teeth together. He's trying to get to me on purpose, trying to make me bite, trying to get me to give him an excuse to kill me – not that he needs one, but he wants a fight. In his sick, perverted head, he wants to goad me into a violent standoff, because that's what gets him off. How could I not have seen this coming? Or did I? Did I see it, but just not care enough? "You disgust me."

"And you excite me."

I try so hard not to, but I cannot help but notice the bulge in his pants. He really is a sick, twisted individual. I spit at his feet. "You want some excitement, come and get it." I aim my gun, firing, but miss.

He jumps at me, knocking me down, taking us both to the dusty ground amid plumes of choking dirt and debris. Landing on my chest, I get the wind knocked out of me, as my gun skids across the floor, lost.

From above me, Rico claws at my jeans, trying to tear them off me.

I struggle, making it difficult for him as I reach into my waistband, pulling a blade from its sheath.

When I plunge the steel into Rico's thigh, I am rewarded with a nightmarish scream.

"Fuck you," I yell, using his weakened state to turn myself over.

Lifting my legs, I kick him in the chest with both feet, making him to topple backward, giving me an opportune moment to right myself.

I stand, shaking, looking over at him as he gets to his knees, his face an angry mask of untainted loathing. Running toward him, crying at the top of my lungs, I hurl my right fist at his face, connecting with his jaw. The impact feels as though it's broken my fingers, so I can imagine it hurt him, too. I hope it did, the fucking bastard.

The warehouse door bursts open and I see armed shadows run passed the racking, the lights from outside silhouetting them.

Turning, I run, taking cover behind pallets of scaffolding struts. Bullets whizz by me, some ricocheting off the metal. I grab for the rifle on my back, readying it. I don't know how many there are in here with me, but I'll fight to take as many of them with me as I can.

Taking a deep breath, I move to show myself, but retake my covered position as the corrugated walls and glass windows are littered with a hail of bullets from outside.

Dying groans and the smell of cordite and copper fill the air. I don't move until the firing stops.

Once I feel it is safe, I poke my head over the pallets, surveying the devastation in front of me. The walls are peppered with holes, light streaming through, highlighting the copious amounts of reflective red pools on the floor. Bodies are strewn all over, at least five. I can't see any sign of Rico, though – motherfucker must have gotten away. Perhaps he's been caught outside.

"Evie?"

My attention is drawn to the warehouse door, where Warren stands, wearing a bulletproof vest, holding a rifle against his chest with both hands.

"Thank god," he breathes, "are you OK?"

It's a redundant question, one I cannot answer, at least not for now. "How did you find me?"

"Your phone," he tells me, "I had it bugged with a tracking device when I went to your hotel room. I glued the back back on, so you wouldn't notice."

Sneaky little bastard. Though, he has just saved my life, so I've got no grounds to complain.

"Where's Rico?"

Warren turns his head, before looking back at me. He's known all along I've been fucking him, but it hurts to see it have such an effect on him.

"He's responsible for my sister. I think she's still alive, and he knows where she is." I don't want Warren thinking that I care for that man anymore. I don't. I want to see him dead, but he has intel that I need. "Is he outside?"

Shaking his head, Warren tells me, "He didn't come out that way."

Fucking wonderful. So, after all of this, he's managed to escape.

I can't take anymore. My legs give out. He's the last hope I have of finding Tessa. If she's really alive, he knows where, and he will go to her. I fear he will kill her, just to get to me. The last shred of hope I have dissipates into a bleak nothingness.

Warren kneels down in front of me, puts his gun down and his arms around me, pulling me close. "We'll find him."

I don't feel the same conviction he appears to. Rico knows I will go looking for him, he will stay off the radar up until a point where he wants to be found. That will likely be after he's killed my sister, so that he can finally deliver her dead body to me and watch me die, both inside and out.

Chapter 19

Warren gives me a ride back to the hotel. No words are spoken between us; I don't want to hear what anyone has to say on the matter. I'm already going to face a shit storm of abuse for breaking protocol, handling things by myself, keeping secrets; so, I could do without the, 'I told you so' speech from Warren on top.

Give my current, low mood, I'm likely to find myself out of job if I dare open my mouth, or retaliate to any crap he tries to give me. I should hope, by now, that Warren knows me well enough not to test me. He understands the sorrow blanketing my heart better than anyone – we were together when it happened – he knows how my sister's disappearance crippled me, turned me ice cold, made me stop giving a fuck about everything.

All of those destructive, excruciating emotions are crushing my body all over again. My insides feel like they're crumbling into burnt, blackened dust. She's alive, and I can't get to her; I can't save her now, just like I couldn't save her before. I have failed her again. I let myself be fooled by the master of manipulation, played like a puppet. My heart has hardened, ready to crack, to take me down once and for all. I deserve everything I am feeling in this moment. I threw caution to the wind, allowed my basic, inner desires to cloud and compromise everything I ever stood for. And for what? For a quick fuck with a man who knew exactly how to hurt me from day one.

I will never forgive myself.

"I'll wait here for you." Warren speaks to me in hushed tones, an air of pity in the atmosphere around us.

I don't want his pity. I don't want his sympathy. I don't want anything from him. I only want my sister back, or be able to die, right beside her, right along with her.

Climbing the stairs to my floor, my mind is consumed with a multitude of images of what Rico might be doing to her, right now. How he might be torturing her for his own sick pleasures, taunting her with everything he's done to me – everything I allowed him to do. The more pain he sees he is inflicting, the more he will continue to goad her, until she begs him to put her out of her misery, as I wish someone would put me out of mine.

My room is cool, but it isn't the reason my body is shaking. Eyeing my bags where I left them, I close the door, unable to move toward them, unable to find the strength to lift them. I slide down the door, crumbling into a sobbing heap.

When I packed my bags earlier, my only thought was that I would be walking out of here, happy in the knowledge that I'd gotten my revenge; the closure that I have waited years for. I would have been able to return home, build bridges with my parents, ensure them that I'd carried out exactly what I'd set out to do for them, for all of us. But I've failed them, too. I can't show my face there.

"I thought I'd have missed this moment."

The blood gushing through my veins turns ice cold. Through teary eyes, I look up, staring into the hideous face of a monster.

"It excites me to know that your misery is my doing." The evil glee in Rico's glare stops my breath.

Stalking forward, he removes his gun from its holster.

This is it, this is the moment I've waited for; the moment I would beg for, if only it wouldn't further fuel his perverted satisfaction. I close my eyes, anticipating the bullet that will end my suffering. I wonder if I will feel it, or whether it will happen too fast for me to register the hot metal buried in my brain. Will I die instantly? Will it hurt? Will I see my sister waiting for me at the end of the tunnel? I've read so many people's accounts of those terrifying moments before they thought death would claim them, how some left their bodies, watching, waiting for their inevitable end, only for it not to come.

The seconds feel like hours. Am I already dead?

Opening my eyes, Rico is still above me, that same malicious sneer plastered across his face. He's been waiting for me to watch, he wants me to see it coming.

When his fist smashes into the side of my skull, rocking my brain, dizzying my vision, I know that he is going to draw this out for as long as he can. As the light fades from the room, I feel him hoist me into his arms. By the time my hotel room door shuts, the black, shredded wings circling me like vultures, swoop down to devour me.

*

I come to my senses before I open my eyes. Keeping them closed, I listen. I can hear the traffic in the distance, but it's muffled by my surroundings. I am somewhere enclosed, small, but hollow. There's an echo all around me, so I cannot pinpoint exactly which direction the road is in.

It appears, however, to be the only sound I can hear, so I open my eyes into slits.

It's dark, but there's a thin strip of light filtering through the bottom of the area in front of me. It's the only light I can detect from inside my prison.

Opening my eyes fully, I can see that I am inside a container, strapped to a chair with what feels like tape – the adhesive is pulling at the fine hairs above my wrists. I struggle against it in an attempt to tear it, give myself at least that small mercy if I am to find myself locked in here.

The clanging of metal scraping against metal from outside, makes me cringe. The door to my confinement opens, allowing penetrating light to flood in. I turn my head away from it, blinding as it is.

"You're awake."

If I never hear his voice again, it will be too soon. "No thanks to you."

"I have something I want to show you." He snakes his hand outside the door, making a grab for something before pulling it in.

My heartbeat increases, my breath catching in my throat.

Tessa.

My sister is bound and gagged, but very much alive. She's skinnier than I remember, her face thin, almost skeletal. Her auburn hair is lank, greasy, her skin pasty; so pale, in fact, that the freckles on her cheeks are more pronounced than I remember them.

Her scrawny arms are covered in track marks, making me feel sick with fury that she's been degraded in such an immoral, depraved way.

I can see her collarbone above the thin nightie she's been forced to wear, the shiny material covered in stains of various sizes and colors.

Tears streak her face, leaving clean trails in all the grim that coats her.

"Tessa." My voice betrays my sorrow, giving away every negative thought or emotion that I have held onto since the day they took her from me.

"We've had some fun, Tessa and me." Rico pulls her closer, exposes her breasts as he kneads it in the palm of his hand, kissing her cheek, even through her fresh tears.

I've never hated someone more than I do right now. I want to bury the sharpest of blades in each of his eyeballs for the way he is looking at her … for the way he has looked at me with that same greedy stare. Only now, it holds a strikingly different meaning.

"Get your fucking paws off her." I writhe in the chair, still desperately trying to free myself. I want to claw through the flesh of his stomach with my bare hands, tear his intestines from him, wrap them tight around his neck and squeeze until he begs me to stop. His life is mine to take, and I want it more than I've ever wanted anything else. "I will kill you." It's a promise I will keep.

His hands roam my sister's body. She tries to shrink away from him, but he pulls her close, holds her with one powerful arm, while the other continues to maul her. "Shall we tell her what we've done, how we feel about each other?" he whispers in her ear, loud enough for me to hear him. "Shall we describe for her, all the ways I have fucked you, every position, every hole? Shall we tell her how much you bled, the first few times? But how much you fucking loved me inside you toward the end?"

My sister's frail body sags, as wracking sobs overwhelm her. Whimpers escape her lips, stifled by the tape covering them.

A scream echoes around the metal container. It erupts from deep within me before I've even registered it. "GET OFF HER!"

I am playing right into his sick, twisted games, but I can't help it; I don't want to hear what he has done to her –

I can see each painful, repulsive moment with every single tear she sheds.

"I've done the same to Evie," he tells her with a smile, "only she loved it from the start. She begged for my hands to touch her, begged for my lips to kiss her, she even begged for my cock deep inside her." He looks at me. "Every time I came inside you, it was because I knew what you didn't. I knew who you were, and you had no idea. You thought I loved you, when all I loved was the idea that I'd been inside both of you, tasted you both, fucked you both until you were screaming. I've never cum so hard."

The next scream that explodes from me hurts my chest. I taste blood, but it's preferential over hearing him relive what will now forever be condemned as my worst nightmare – moments etched in my mind's eye for a lifetime, moments that will burn through my core with the heat of a thousand hell fires.

With a strength that belies my stature, powered only by the pure adrenaline streaming through my veins, I break free of my bonds. Launching myself off the chair, I collide with Rico, taking him down to the ground with me.

Above him, I pummel his face with both fists. The red spatters become a blur, his face a pulpy mass of broken flesh. Behind me, my sister screams, cries for me to kill him, to end this for the both of us, finally.

Rico forces his body up. His regained vigor is no match for mine, and I fall away from him, cracking the side of my head off a sharp corner of the container.

Dazed, I try to stand, but Rico boots me in the ribs. Pain shoots through me like hot needles, taking my breath away. I'm thrown against the metal walls, winded, my back against the cold steel.

Rico crouches in front of me, the leer on his face made more gruesome by the blood congealed around the lacerations I've caused. "Even now, you still turn me on."

Tessa – still bound – hurls herself at him, but she is too small and weak to make any difference; Rico bats her off of him like a fly. She squeals, landing in a heap on the floor, howling for him to stop.

He turns his attention back to me, reaching out his hands, gripping my throat. "I think you enjoyed this last time."

Something tells me I'm not going to like it much this time around, though.

White stars dance in my vision, the tighter his hold becomes. I hear my blood gushing through my ears. My chest burns with the increased pressure to suck in air, my head is on the verge of exploding, my brain pumping against the side of my skull as panic grips me vice-tight.

Fumbling in my boot, I find the handle of the blade I so badly need. But my fingers are losing the feeling in them; I struggle to gain a proper grip.

Using my last ounce of strength, before I succumb to the pain, I will my fingers to close around the hilt; I beg them to do this one last thing for me. With a jolt, they find the strength within them, grabbing hold of the handle, pulling it from my boot.

Before the fight ebbs from me, I fling my hand up, aiming high. The sharp, glinting blade embeds itself in the soft flesh just below Rico's ear.

His eyes widen, his body stops.

I twist the knife, pushing it in further, further still, until it is hilt-deep.

Rico's body goes into spasm, he falls to the side, his arms and legs twitching.

I spit on his dying body, watching the gleaming pool of crimson spread out beneath him. "Bet you can't go as deep at that, asshole. I win, you lose." I watch him take his last breath, satisfied that he is finally dead.

"Eve?"

She's the only one who's ever called me Eve – I never thought I'd hear it again.

Standing on shaky legs, I walk over to my sister, seeing the half-torn off tape still attached to her face. I drop to my knees before her, tears drenching my face, drowning out the last two years' worth of heartache, hopelessness and sorrow. Pulling her close, I cling on to her, refusing to let her go in case this is all a dream. She's finally back in my arms, in my life. Only now, can I appreciate everything I have done, everything I have lost, everything I have sacrificed. It's all been for this moment.

My entire body shudders through the cries of joy; I wail like a banshee, not giving a fuck who might hear. My throat is sore, my voice gravelly, it hurts to cry, but if it means having my sister back, I will gladly put up with it for the rest of my natural life.

"Eve," my sister says, again, "the other girls."

My mind dominated with her return to me, I wonder what she means, finally understanding as I take in her haggard appearance. The other girls – the one's Dieter spoke of, the ones shipped yesterday. "They're here?"

She nods, using my shoulders to help her stand.

Rising to my own feet, I let her use my body to support herself, as we both hobble out of the container.

We're in a closed-off yard, surrounded by rusted containers piled high. Rubbish and scrap litter the floor in this abandoned area. In front of us, is a white lorry. I know they're in there; it doesn't take a genius to work that out.

Limping over, the pain in my ribs still palpable, I grab hold of the locking mechanism. With a loud racket, I push it to the side, throwing up the rumbling shutter. I recoil at the sickening stick.

Whimpers and small murmurs echo inside, emitted from the twenty or so girls inside, as they shuffle to the back of the van, petrified, clinging to one another. I knew this wouldn't be a pretty sight, but I am not prepared for I'm staring at.

One of the girls moves forward, into the light, using a hand to shield to bright rays of the sun from her tired, lean face. She is a bloody mess; dirty, tear-stained. She can't be any older than sixteen, and my body shudders at the thought of what could have been in store for her.

Each of the girls behind her are similarly filthy, all but skin and bone. Their clothes are torn, some are naked, bruised, their hair a bedraggled mess. Their glassy eyes are red and puffy from tears they still cry.

They've all endured something so harrowing, it doesn't bear thinking about – beaten black and blue, drugged, abused. Their treatment is something I have thought about every day for the past two years, knowing that Tessa would have gone through the same. It's eaten me from the inside out, destroyed my will, consumed my being. I haven't been able to stomach this level of evil, so I can only imagine how this will affected these girls in front of me.

It's not much, but it gives me some pleasure to be able to tell them, "You're going to be OK."

From above us, the whirring of helicopter blades allows me to breathe a sigh of relief. It's over.

At least for these girls.

There are still hundreds out there in need of rescuing.

It's why I will continue to do what I do. This personal experience has taught me much about myself that I didn't know. I am tainted, there is blood on my hands, but it will only serve to strengthen my will from now on.

Despite everything, knowing that families will be reunited with their loved ones – knowing that *I* will be able to walk back into my family home with Tessa at my side – is enough to know that, whatever I must do, whatever I have to sacrifice, it's all worth it in …

... THE END

Want to read more by Blair Coleman?

Here's a snippet from Graceful Damnation:

Chapter 1

London, August 2012

Grace

Walking into work, I keep my head down; my hair covering most of my face, while I head for the staff toilet.

"Afternoon, Gracie," my boss, Ivan calls from somewhere behind the counter.

I throw him a wave, but don't look up.

Shouldering my way into the bathroom, I lock the door behind me. Only then do I lift my head and look into the mirror above the sink.

The daft bastard has marked my fucking face - on any other day, he tries to avoid leaving bruises where people can see and question; calls them nosey twats for prying.

But what does he expect? If he punches me in the face for all the world to see, I'm gonna get the Spanish Inquisition from those close to me - which basically consists of my boss and the other evening waitress, Penny.

Delving into my bag, I pull out my foundation and dab it on my face, trying to hide the rainbow of colours coming through.

"Can I borrow you for a minute, Gracie?" Ivan's voice rings out from the other side of the door.

"Won't be a mo." Time to put my game face on.

Shit, that'll have to do - I can hide the majority with my hair and just hope no-one picks up on it.

Leaving the toilet, I follow my pudgy, bald-headed boss into the café, keeping the swollen side of my face out of Ivan's line of sight.

"What can I get you?" I stroll up to the customer Ivan points out and take my order pad from the pocket of my apron.

Looking at me, a smile breaks across his face, "What you offering, darling?" He places a rough hand on my lower arm and begins to stroke. I flinch at the contact, despite being used to his platonic affection.

"I'm offering not to break your fingers, provided you remove your hand within the next three seconds." I throw him my usual sugary-sweet smile and bat my lashes, even as I try to slow my erratic heart-rate.

The guy's a regular, always in here around this time and always hitting on either me or Penny. He doesn't take offence and always laughs at my quips, and tonight is no different.

"I'll take a coffee, thanks, sweetheart. Creamy and sweet, just like my favourite hostess." His grin widens.

Returning his smile, I cock my head, "Now, would that be me, or the other girl you salivate over?"

"Only have eyes for you, babe." He winks at me.

"Uh-huh, for tonight, at least."

*

It's nearing closing, and I know Penny's noticed my face – she's been staring at me on and off all night, and she'll be on me the moment I hang my apron up.

It won't be for a while yet, however, because a swarm of people walk in – fresh from last orders at the pub opposite, I imagine.

Running up behind me, Penny slaps my arse. "I have those papers you asked about. You up for a quick drink when we're done?"

She's giving me her code for, 'and we need to talk about your face, again', but I can't.

"I wish I could, babe, but I need to get back."

Pouting and running a hand through her cropped, blond hair, she murmurs, "Grace... ." She looks at me with large, brown, doe-eyes – a knowing expression. "Fine, we'll have a quick one here when we lock the doors, and I'm not taking no for an answer."

"Alright, but just the one; I have to be up early tomorrow."

*

Forty-five minutes later, the café doors are locked, Ivan's left and Penny pulls a bottle of vodka from her bag, smiling while she shakes it at me, motioning for me to grab two tumblers.

We each take a seat and she pours me a double measure, sliding it across the table to me. "What happened this time, Grace?" She doesn't look at me while she pours herself one.

"What do you mean?" I don't look up - don't want her to focus on my face, but I figure she's already taken a good look at it and that's why we're sitting here.

"You know what I mean, lady." She releases a heavy sigh, twirling the silver heart pendant she's wearing around her neck - I bought it for her birthday last year. "I have those documents you wanted." She knocks back the vodka and reaches for her bag.

My voice is barely a whisper when I reply, "Thank you, Penny. I couldn't do this without you." She hands me the forged travel documents and papers and I slide them down the side of my top, securing them beneath the strap of my bra.

"Grace Emery, sorry, Morgan; I'm going to miss you, ya know?" Her eyes sag with sadness and she bites the inside of her cheek.

"I'll miss you, too, babe." A tear falls down my cheek and Penny wipes it away with a half-smile.

This weekend, I'll be outta here - three days and I will be as far from London as humanly possible.

You see, four years ago, when I was twenty years old, my boyfriend, Garrett Phillips walked into my life.

After years of enduring a shitty upbringing following the death of my parents before I hit my teens, I ended up on the streets and a breath away from selling my body in order to pay for a decent meal. But then a thirty-one year old Garrett walked into my life and changed things for me. He offered me a place to stay and I moved in with him.

A week later, he fucked me up good. Blackened my eye, bruised my ribs and fractured two fingers because he thought he caught me eyeing up his cousin.

The beatings became a regular thing and you're probably wondering why I didn't just leave him.

He provided for me, took me off the streets and saved me from a hooker's life. He gave me a home when no-one else would. I didn't know any different, and, at the time, I feared leaving him would cost me more than one or two fractured bones. I know what Garrett can do to someone who crosses him. Over the years, I've watched him beat the living crap out of people he called friends. I knew he'd kill me if he ever found me.

I got my job working for Ivan at a local greasy spoon about two years ago. Garrett doesn't like it. Could be because I make my own money, but more than likely because guys can hit on me when he's not around. To appease him - or rather because he beat me for saying no – I've been dealing for him on the side. It's been a huge risk, because if Ivan found out, he'd have kicked me out of the place and I needed this job so badly. But it'll all be over soon.

Garrett's been taking the money for the drugs, and my wages - at least, he thinks he has been. For the past year, I've been lying to him about how much I make; keeping back my tips so that I'll be able to leave him and go somewhere he can't find me.

I'll change my name, my appearance, anything if it means I can get away.

By the time Ivan pays me at the end of this week, I'll have enough. I figure I'll go somewhere like Scotland, or maybe even Ireland - somewhere far enough away the lazy fuck won't bother to come looking for me.

I'll miss Penny. She's been a lifeline for me while we've worked for Ivan, but she knows I can't tell her where I'm going – she knows I will have to cut all ties from this life. I can't take the risk.

I stand and give her the tightest hug I can, crying into her shoulder and telling her how much she will always mean to me.

*

It's gone midnight by the time I'm stumbling down my street, but my brain's fuzzy from the vodka we knocked back in the last half hour, so I'm not too bothered right now.

I have a smile on my face because I've taken my shoes off, and the warm, rough pavement is providing a delicious massage to the ache in my feet. I'm struggling to keep my eyes open, though, when I turn into the shared garden of our apartment block – I'll be in bed before I know it.

Bending down to get a close-up of the lock, I slip my key in – making sure to be quiet – and walk into the living room.

Garrett's slouched, eyes lolling, in his favourite, brown leather armchair; that thing has seen better days

– the leather's worn across the arms where he picks at it when he's high on his choice drug of the day. It's also full of knife holes where he's lost his temper more than a few times and took it out on the furniture.

His three-day old, brown stubble is showing the grey his shaved head doesn't and he's squinting his beady, green eyes at something on the TV, with a joint jammed between his thin lips.

Turning his listless, glazed eyes on me, he gets up – drowsy and stumbling – throwing what's left of the spliff to the floor and stomping it out.

"Where the fuck you been?" He spits his words through gritted teeth and my stomach plummets.

My eyes dart around the room, catching sight of two of Garrett's gang buddies – Billy 'Brass' Brassington and Garrett's cousin, Frankie Davis – on the opposite, garish orange, three-seater sofa.

They're both staring at me, sneering, decaying teeth on display while they knock back their cans of Carling.

Garrett's fist connects with my cheek and I fall to the floor, spitting blood. "Been fucking your way around Croydon, have you?" He gets in my face, nose to nose; his putrid-smelling spittle coating my lips and nose.

Leaning up on two hands, I turn my head toward him. “No, Garrett. I promise. We had a last min–“

He slaps me hard, despite his dazed state. “Lying bitch, I can smell the booze on your breath.”

“Penny and I had one drink after work, after the rush.” My voice quaking, I don’t dare look at him this time, but I won’t cry – I never give him that satisfaction.

The kick he launches into my ribs is clumsy, but heavy and he staggers while I drop to the floor again. “You better be telling the fuckin’ truth, Gracie. You know what I’ll do to you if you’re dishing out pussy to every bastard goin’.”

Brass throws a can at my head, “Fetch me another.”

“Guzzling fucker,” Garrett slurs, eyes half-closed, backing away and slumping in his chair.

Taking a couple of deep, painful breaths I clamber to my feet, clutching at the ache lancing through my ribs. I look between Garrett and Brass.

Brass – like Frankie – is disgusting to look at; both gangly and gaunt, in comparison to Garrett’s bulky frame, but with receding hairlines and sunken eyes. That's what years of drug abuse will do to you.

Garrett reckons he's clever; only dabbles now and again in the 'softer' stuff, not the hardcore shit he deals – plus he's a greedy fucker, it would take a miracle for him to lose his timber.

I don't say a word to either of them; instead, I limp into the kitchen and grab another cold one from the fridge.

After a few minutes staring into the veiling darkness outside the kitchen window, I shuffle back in on the threadbare, cream carpet, dropping Brass's can on him – daft fucker is already half-asleep, doesn't even notice the can falling into his lap. Frankie's head leans on Brass's shoulder, drooling.

Garrett's dozed off, too, *thank fuck.* I spy the remains of some 'new' drug they've likely been smoking all night. With any luck, I'll manage a couple of hour's kip before Garrett crashes and decides he needs to get his dick wet.

His head falls back against the chair, mouth open, letting out soft snores.

Creeping out of the room and down the hallway, I dodge the squeaky floorboards I've committed to memory.

Entering the bathroom, I glare at the grime across the walls and floor, fags ends litter the sink and toilet and there is tin foil and baggies thrown across every available surface – some empty, some not.

Looking in the mirror, I note the purple and red bruise already forming against my pale skin, accentuated further by my bright, auburn hair and the charcoal rings circling my once-sparkling, baby blue eyes.

This would be another one of the times where Garrett's been too high to remember not to mark my face. I'm going to have to make up yet another excuse tomorrow at work. Maybe I'll just call in sick.

Light footsteps sound in the corridor and I peer out the door.

"Hey, Frankie." Garrett's cousin ambles toward me.

He doesn't say anything, just leers at me, shouldering the wall while he stumbles forward. I'm used to his stares, he's always glaring at me one way or another, often with a look that says he wants in my pants – I ignore it, lest Garrett accuses me of flirting again.

Closing the gap, his eyes narrow at me, his lip hitching into a half-sneer before he pushes me further into the bathroom, closing the door behind him.

"Gaz is sleeping, I'm gonna keep you satisfied tonight." His breath stinks of beer and stale cigarettes.

"Leave it out, Frankie." I go for the doorknob, my hand shaking.

Thrusting his hand against my chest, he shoves me against the basin and it hurts, jarring my tailbone and sending a shooting pain up my spine.

"Frankie, what the fuck, man?" Terror seeps into my trembling voice. I don't shout out though, I'll be the one paying the price for *my* 'infidelity' if I do.

"Shut up; let a real man show you how it's done." His rancid breath makes me want to wretch. "You're gorgeous, you know that?" He runs a scrawny hand down my cheek and I flinch.

Patting my face a little too hard, he moves, wasting no time unbuckling his belt. I'm shaking like a leaf, but I'm not standing for this – dealing with one piece of shit from this family is enough – *Frankie isn't having his way with me, too.*

I muster the strength to push him back with leaden limbs and try to walk past. He stumbles over his half-removed jeans, but reaches out for me.

"Whore!" he spits at me.

A shooting pain races through my neck when he grabs my shoulder-length hair and yanks me back.

Bile rises up my throat and he smashes my head in the mirror above the basin with an audible crack. Blinking back the sharp pain, I catch blurred sight of slivers tumbling from the frame and into the sink. I hold onto the basin, stumbling, nicking my feet on the larger shards that have dropped onto the linoleum floor, fighting for control of my watery vision.

Warm blood trickles down my neck before Frankie grabs the side of my head, turns me and forces me on my knees. He flops his limp dick out of his pants and grabs a fistful of my hair, angling my head toward it.

It smells like he hasn't washed the thing in weeks.

He growls and my stomach lurches when he hurls me against the side of the bathtub, and I hiss through gritted teeth at the agony while I clamber to my knees. It's that cheap, plastic shit; otherwise it could've done some serious damage. I blocked the impact with my shoulder, but it jarred my ribs all the same.

He drops down in front of me and spits in my face. Thick, stinking mucus slides down my cheek. "I been waiting on this for years. I'm gonna fuck you six ways from Sunday, bitch."

He grabs me around the throat and throws me to the floor, my heart pounding in my ears. I struggle against him – body stinging from the lacerations to my exposed flesh from the glass slivers beneath me. He tears at the shorts I wear under my uniform.

"You're gonna get it now, open those legs for Frankie." He leers over me, his lips curling up.

He painfully manhandles my breast, trying to pry my legs apart while I tremble beneath his weight. I open my mouth to scream, but he clamps a sweaty palm over me and I can taste the cigarettes on his skin.

My eyes bulge, staring at the grimacing shadow of his face, silhouetted by the light above.

Panic constricts me when his fingers probe the thin material of my knickers, my chest tightens and I grind my teeth into Frankie's hand. I feel the pinch of skin between my teeth and bite down, hard. Frankie yelps, removes his hand from my face and backhands me with it.

It stings like a bitch and I spit blood on the floor, clutching my cheek with one hand, battling Frankie with the other.

Kneeling on my wrist – his bone grating against mine with excruciating pain – he continues to rain blows down on my face, not just stopping at a few bitch slaps.

Frankie grabs me by the waist and yanks me down, making light work of ripping off my underwear. I try to scream again, but he cracks me another blow and my head snaps sideways.

The glint of a long, glass shard catches my eye.

The perverted tosser positions himself to shove his semi-erect cock inside me, pushing my legs further apart and jarring my hip bone. He thrusts forward, trying to angle himself in, but I don't give him the satisfaction.

I grab the sharp sliver – shredding my palm in the process – and ram the pointed end straight into the side of his neck.

The glass slices like a knife through butter.

Frankie's hand flies to the weapon. He pulls it out – blood spurting across the floor – and clamps his hand over his neck. Thick, dark fluid runs between his fingers.

I scramble back, feet slipping in the blood seeping from his wound. Quick jets spatter my clothes and face. I close my eyes and mouth – no way is that shit getting into my system; I've no idea what the dirty bastard's got swimming in his.

Frankie drops to the side, flapping and flailing like a fish out of water. Scurrying back on hands and feet, I watch his eyes roll back, his face turning ashen. Slick blood pumps from his neck while he tries to keep his palm over it. It pools beneath him in a deep, crimson puddle.

Spasms subsiding, his arms drop, limp. His bloodied face has fallen to the side and his tongue is half-hanging out. Vacant, glassy eyes stare at nothing.

Panic settles in my churning gut and the realisation of my actions hit me like a sledgehammer to my stomach. On wooden limbs, I lurch for the tub and hurl over the polished enamel.

Wiping my mouth with the back of my hand, I rise on shaky legs, averting my gaze from Frankie's lifeless form.

Naked from the waist down – and past giving a fuck – I stagger down the hallway, uniform bunched around my hips. Pangs of agony shoot through my body and I remember the first creaky floorboard the moment it groans under my weight.

Shit! Standing stock still, I listen. I can't hear anything save for Garrett's bull-like snoring and the buzzing of muffled voices on the TV.

Ambling forward, I grip the doorframe and peer into the sitting room, leaving smeared, red handprints on the yellowing paint. Garrett is still sound asleep and Brass is muttering something incoherent to himself in between snorts and snores.

I swallow down a large lump of bile and lumber back down the hallway, noticing the dark drops and bloody footprints I've left on the grey carpet. *Fuck,* I don't have time to clean this shit up.

Passing the bathroom, I see Frankie's limp foot poking from behind the door and my legs give out. I drop to the floor, heaving; my body wracked with sobs, my head throbbing. I close my eyes and suck in deep breaths, my mind ticking over, scrambling for a coherent thought.

Clambering to my feet, I stumble into the bedroom, eyes darting about for clothes while pain lances through my neck and back.

Throwing on some track bottoms – my breath coming in intermittent gulps – I shuck off my pinafore, the envelope still tucked inside my bra, and pull on a hoodie, wincing, trying to ignore the torture surging through every bone in my body.

I wipe my hands and face with a top from the floor before I wrap the bloodied material around my palm.

I grab a backpack from the battered, old wardrobe and begin shoving clothes into it, along with the cash I've been hoarding in our beat-up mattress and a stash Garrett keeps hidden he thinks I know nothing about.

Tiptoeing down the corridor, careful to check Garrett is still out cold, I prize the door open with infinite slowness – sweat beading my forehead, limbs throbbing. I stagger out into the sticky, humid, summer air – thankful for the darkness – and head for the tube station, not once glancing back.

Chapter 2
Chicago, October 2014

Grace

"Fuck, you lucky bitch!"

Harley laughs at my outburst. She's just shot me in the head, again!

We're playing Call of Duty on two separate TVs in the same large, bare-bricked living room in our loft apartment, so I can't see when she sneaks up and offs me. She's too damn good at this game.

"You need to get some practice in, Gray." Her accent isn't Chicago; she's from Tennessee, and it's clear.

Scoffing at her remark, I smile. She's such a tomboy and I love her to bits for it.

Two years ago, I got lucky – very fucking lucky. Terrified the police would find me, I ran and ran, and I didn't stop until I reached Heathrow airport.

Using the fake documents Penny gave me, I booked a flight to Chicago – I'd literally closed my eyes in front of a map and jabbed my finger down on the sparkling city in Illinois. After what happened, Scotland or Ireland seemed too close to home.

The beauty captivated me the moment I stepped off the bus from the airport to the city – the tall buildings, the dazzling lights. The air felt clean and fresh.

Staying in meagre shelters across the city for the first three months, I worked in and out of bars for cash in hand. Everyone I encountered seemed so friendly, willing to help – a far cry from the calibre of people I associated with in London.

In my free time, I began creating sculptures from salvaged rubbish, used my money to buy paints and canvases, and started selling my work around local parks and in the bars I worked in. I found it therapeutic, and I gained quite a knack for the craft.

A little over a year ago, photographer Harley Lewis walked into my bar. She took one look at me and my work, heard my London accent, and would not shut up with her millions of questions about England and my life there.

Avoiding the obvious answers, we took to one another right away. She offered me a place to stay with her and her model roommate, Cameron Edwards.

Harley helped me set up my own website selling my sculptures and paintings, and I do well through it – a natural flair she calls it. I am so grateful for her and Cam.

Harley drops her controller and slides over the teakwood floor toward me. Her long, chocolate waves pool over her shoulders and cascade down her back.

She places a gentle hand on my shoulder, "You want something to drink?" she asks me, bunching my hair in her palm.

She's always fiddling with something, and she loves the colour of my tresses, so she's always playing with them – I'm not uncomfortable with it, I find it sisterly, the way she does it.

I shake my head. "I'm good thanks, babe."

"So, you picked anything to wear for Saturday, yet?" There's a smile in her words.

It's Harley's twenty-sixth birthday Saturday, and Cam has managed to score us tickets to some hot new club opening in town – God bless his good looks and model connections. Harley might be a tomboy, but she still loves to dress up all glitz and glam. I call her a geezer-bird in my common London accent and she laughs at me when I say it.

"Chill out, Harl, it's only Monday; plenty of time for that."

She giggles and I can't help but smile.

Placing my controller down, I switch off the games console just before our front door opens and I hear high-pitched squeals and giggles.

God give me strength, Cam has brought home a 'date' and it's not even dinner time yet.

He's got commitment issues, our Cam, and I accept that – I'm not exactly falling all over myself to enter another relationship... though if the right guy came along... but it kills Harley when he brings these empty-headed, bimbo tramps back to our apartment.

Her eyes are glued to the raven-haired doll – whose sole personality is, without a doubt, in her inflated chest – hanging off Cam's arm. Harl looks ready to cry – her eyes are welling up.

Cam doesn't know Harley is crushing on him big time. Ha, listen to me – fancies him. He could at least have some damn respect, though, and not subject us to his raucous fucking – this is a loft apartment, not a damn mansion – we can hear almost everything bouncing off the brick and metal-lined walls.

I glance at Harley and the longing in her eyes while she moves her stare to Cam.

Oblivious, he smiles at us both, grabs the chuckling, caked-in-make-up floozy by the hand, and drags her to his room.

I lift my arse off the plush, red sofa and walk up to Harley, placing my hand in the middle of her back. "Come on, babe, we'll hit Potter's."

Potter's Lounge is a bar a couple of minutes' walk from our apartment. It's decked out in dark wood floors, red and brown leather and low lighting. It oozes old-school Chicago appeal.

Harley doesn't need asking twice. She throws a leather jacket over her casual jeans-tank top combo and heads for the door.

I reach for my light blazer and rush out after her, grabbing the door keys.

"Why does he do it, Gray?" She links my arm and rests her head on my shoulder while we walk.

"Because he doesn't know you like him, hun."

"But why *those* kinds of women; they're vile?" She wrinkles her nose up.

"But they're easy, and he's clueless. You need to tell him, babe." I'm sympathetic toward her, but she really does need to man up and let it out.

"I'm not his type, though. I'm too *man-like*. He'll laugh in my face and our friendship will be ruined." She lets out a hefty sigh.

"Oh, Harl. Don't you get how fabulous you are? He'd be thick as shit to knock you back."

"But what if he does?"

I don't have an answer for her, but luckily we're just strolling through the entrance of Potter's.

We grab a seat at the bar and order two Turkey Clubs and beers.

*

An hour rolls by, and Harley and I have forgotten about slagging Cam's choice of women off and are busy giggling over the slightest of things – courtesy of the alcohol, no doubt.

The barman approaches us and hands over two more bottles.

"We didn't order these, barkeep," I giggle, falling into Harley's arm and causing her to burst out laughing.

"Barkeep!" she screams out, banging her palm on the dark, shining bar top and laughing out loud.

Thankfully, the barman, Dane, takes my unintended insult in good humour and smirks. He's cute when he smiles; it dimples his cheeks and highlights his blue eyes.

"Courtesy of the gentleman at the end of the bar." Dane grins at us, pointing to his left.

I glance over and a good-looking guy tilts his beer bottle in our direction.

Hmm, tasty. I can make out his dazzling green eyes from all the way over here, and his dirty blonde hair is a funky-styled mess.

I return his gorgeous smile and tip my head in thanks, taking a sip of the gifted beverage.

"He's yummy," Harley slurs, a little too loudly. The guy's smile widens. "You should ask for his number."

I throw my glance back in her direction. "Harley--"

"No, no, no." The drink is taking its toll on her. "I don't think I've seen you go on a date since you moved in and you need to get laid, girl."

I palm my head. This girl is unreal when she's tipsy.

Little does she realise, I *choose* not to date. It's not that I don't feel ready – enough time has passed for me to adjust – it's just that... well, I don't quite know for sure, maybe I'm just being skeptical... guarded, even. It's gonna take more than a couple of beers and a dazzling smile to win me over. I think.

"I agree," a male voice begins, "about taking my number, I mean; not that you need to get laid... I wouldn't know."

I turn my head and the hot bloke has moved closer to us. He is rather delicious and he smells of ginger, woody musk and spice - an inebriating scent.

"Grace." I offer the guy my hand in an effort to stop him stumbling over his words, and because I *might* be interested... in nothing more than a drink, mind. For now.

"Miles," he returns, collecting himself. His large, warm hand engulfs my petite one.

"Harley." She shoves her hand between us, almost spilling my beer over poor Miles. She doesn't apologize. "Why are you sat alone?" No inhibitions, this one.

Smiling, he looks to her, "I was with a buddy, but he left not long ago. I saw you gorgeous ladies and figured I'd worm my way in with a free beer. How am I doing?" He cocks a smile and winks at me.

"Fabulous." Harl takes a long pull on her gratuitous drink and gives Miles a thumbs up before the bottle pops off her lips. "Grace needs a man."

Closing my eyes for a quick moment, I envisage all the ways I could get the bitch back for this.

"Sorry about her." I jerk my head in Harl's direction. "She's a lightweight." I punch her in the leg.

"Ouch! Ho!" She counters with a jab to my upper arm, laughing.

"That's OK," Miles snickers, "I think she might be onto something."

"You think I need a man?" I suppress a smile and raise an eyebrow. I gotta hand it to him – he's got a knack for putting his foot in it.

"No! Shit, sorry. I didn't... oh, fuck." He averts his gaze and stares into his beer.

A laugh rumbles in my chest and I place a hand against his taut bicep. "It's OK, Miles. I get what you mean."

He tries for a smile while Harley giggles into her beer bottle next to me, her eyes squeezed closed when I try to throw her a wide-eyed glare.

I turn back. "Listen, Miles, we appreciate the beers, but this really is girl time, ya know?" I raise my eyebrows and cast him a quirky, half-smile hopefully conveying the universal indicator for, 'we're slagging off men'. "But give me your number and I'll call you."

He smiles at me, understanding I think, and jots his digits down on a napkin before handing them to me. His fingers brush mine sending a few tingles down south.

"Make sure you do, Grace." He recovers from his embarrassment before downing the remains of his beer and placing his warm, moistened lips against my cheek. I shudder. "I'll look forward to it."

Watching him - or rather his tight arse - walk out the door, I smile to myself.

"You shoulda hit that," Harley pipes up, curbing her amusement.

I laugh at her and tell her to hush before taking a sip from my bottle.

*

It's well past one in the morning by the time we stumble back into the apartment. Cam is sitting on the sofa watching *The Walking Dead* DVD Harley got him for his twenty-fifth birthday a few months back.

"Hey ladies," he chimes, turning to smirk at us and pausing his show.

"Barbie gone home?" Harley's voice takes on a honeyed tone while she bats her eyelids.

Cam jumps over the back of the couch and races up to Harley, grabbing her in a bear hug. "What's up Harbo, you jealous?"

Oh, the poor boy. He has no idea.

"Hell no! Now put me down, ya great buffoon."

Cam places Harl back on her feet and she smacks his chest, mumbling something under her breath that sounds like, “ass”.

“Yes, *Candy* has gone home.”

I snort. “You’re fucking with us, right? Candy?”

Cam grins and shrugs his shoulders. Harley glowers at him. I really do wish she’d just tell him how she feels.

Despite his ‘playboy’ lifestyle – and admittedly it isn’t *that* bad, maybe two or three girls every couple of months – he is an amazing person.

Yeah, he’s a model, and he’s nothing short of stunning with dark hair that falls over deep, chocolate eyes and a tall, muscled physique, but he knows it’s not all about his looks. He volunteers at homeless shelters and entertains sick kids at the local hospital. He’s a saint, but none of it goes to his head – he’s so laid back and humble. It’s easy to see why Harley likes him. But a guy’s got needs, and Harley is keeping schtum over her infatuation with him.

“I’m going to bed.” It’s time I left Harley and Cam alone – not that anything will come of it.

Making my way down the hall to my room, I hear Harley rustling in the kitchen and Cam starting his DVD back up. I roll my eyes and shake my head, smiling.

I don't bother switching the light on, I just undress and throw myself into bed. I always used to like sleeping in my underwear when I was a kid because I loved the feel of the soft duvet on my skin.

When I slept like this back in London, Garrett would take the opportunity to fuck me – in any hole he saw fit – and I hated it. Keeping clothes on meant restricted access unless he undressed me, and – on the occasion he didn't beat me into submission or literally rip my clothes away from me – he usually didn't have the patience, or fell asleep before finishing.

It took me months after moving in here before I felt comfortable and secure enough to do this again, and I smile while I snuggle under the covers, appreciating the soft scratches of the fabric on my naked body.

The last thing I hear, before I shut my eyes to welcome oblivion is Harley scream, "Go fuck yourself, Cammy." Then her bedroom door slams shut.

Wonder what he said this time. I'll ask her tomorrow.

Chapter 3
Grace

My alarm goes off at six-thirty and I really wish I'd remembered to turn it off the night before.

My head is swimming a little from the previous night's beers and I take a minute for the room to stop spinning before I attempt to sit up.

Today is going to be busy – I need to fetch Harley's birthday cake, go dress shopping for Saturday and finish a project for a client who's commissioned me to do four Impressionist canvases for her law office downtown – business is good.

Leaning against the headboard, I inhale. I can already smell fresh coffee brewing, so someone is clearly more insane than I am to be up at this hour.

Stretching my legs out in front of me, I groan amid creaking bones and bedframe. Swinging over the side, I put my feet on the luxurious, beige carpet and ball my toes in the plush fabric. I've done this every day for a year just because I can.

I smile and get up, throwing a long T-shirt on before padding into the living room.

Cameron is rattling around the open-plan kitchen in nothing but a pair of track bottoms, and his banging is making my head pound.

"Cammy, you wanna keep the decibels down to somewhere near jackhammer level?" I moan at him, secretly appreciating his smooth, toned abs from the corner of my eye.

"Hey, gorgeous. Heavy night last night?" He grins at me and I throw the tea-towel beside me at his head. He catches it and sticks out his tongue.

"Your fault." I accuse.

He feigns insult and gapes at me. "I beg your pardon, missy? The way I hear it, you got yourself some action last night, too."

"I so did not!" I'll kill Harley when she emerges from her tomb.

"Not what I heard." His smile, and the waggle of his eyebrows, tell me he's pulling my leg, so I ignore him for now.

"What else did you and Harl discuss? She didn't sound too happy when she went to bed."

"No idea, Graybo," he shrugs, "I gave her another dig about her jealous streak; obviously I was joking, but she took it the wrong way, I suppose."

"Oh, Cammy." I roll my eyes at him and laugh.

"What?"

Shaking my head, I pour myself a coffee.

Ignoring his question, I ask him, "You going downtown today? I could do with a lift to pick up Harl's cake."

He nods, taking a sip of his drink, holding up his hand indicating he'll be leaving in five.

I take my coffee back into my bedroom to throw some clothes on, making sure to be ready when he is.

Exiting Cam's stunning, silver, Toyota FT-86, I turn to thank him. He waves at me before revving off to whatever shoot he's got going on today.

I step into the Bakery on N Wabash Ave and greet Bella, the chef who can perform pastry miracles, in my honest opinion.

"Hey, Gracie-Baby, you come for your cake?" She's so cheerful, it almost hurts my head.

"Sure am, Bella-Honey, thanks for doing this, you're a legend." I offer her my most appreciative smile.

"You're welcome, sugar. Here she is." She pulls a pink and white box with a white, rope handle from under the counter and shows me her masterpiece.

I love it, it's spot on – a PlayStation controller. Harley is going to freak when she sees it.

"This is perfect, babe." I take the culinary delight and offer endless thanks and appreciation before I leave.

My heads all but in the clouds; I'm stoked with Harl's cake. She's gonna love it so much. Crossing the road, I jump at the sound of screeching tires before a horn blasts from behind me. Sidestepping quickly back onto the pavement, I watch the black limo catch the side of my cake box and it goes flying through the air.

Everything slows. The car stops and the box lands on the floor where cake explodes all across the road and all up my clothes.

I see red, I am fuming. Before I've even thought about it, I grab a piece of the obliterated confection and I launch it at the limo. It thuds against the back window and detonates across the blacked-out glass.

"Stupid twat!" I scream, beyond giving a shit at the passers-by, stood staring at the fiasco. Not one of the fuckers asks if I'm OK, though.

The back-passenger door opens and a suited and booted leg exits, followed by the rest of what I can only describe as a light-haired, broad, muscled Adonis. A few muffled sounds filter into my subconscious – something about speeding, accident... I'm not entirely too sure because *Holy Hell!* I am left breathless. My almost-vehicular-manslaughter-er saunters over, going for imposing by striding over to me with purpose. I'm not giving him any leeway to berate me with his shit, though, when I see him open his mouth to say something.

"What the hell are you playing at?" I yell at him.

He slows, and eyes me up and down. "You're British," he points out.

Obviously. "No shit, dickhead," I yell, "and you almost fucking killed me."

I'm not clued up on all American accents, but he sounds like he's from Upstate New York, not Chicago.

Regardless, his voice is dreamy and for a moment I forget to be angry – I think my knees might be wobbling and I want to run my fingers over the light stubble on his defined jaw...

"And what about this shit?" I point to the mess at my feet. "How am I supposed to replace this? I had it custom made!" He might be fit as hell, but he's ruined my damn cake – I don't care if I wasted money on it, it's the time I don't have to get another made.

"Please, allow me to have that seen to, Miss... ?"

"I had to wait over a week for it, you can't just 'see to it'. I need it for the weekend."

"I can't apologise enough, Miss... ?"

I'm not telling him my name, he can come at it from every angle imaginable, but he's not getting it.

"Forget it." I throw my hands in the air and stomp past him. He's completely ruined my goddamn day, I'm not even in the mood to go shopping any more, and I'm still dressed in fucking cake!

*

Walking into the apartment, I see Harley in the living room playing Call of Duty – surprise, surprise. She pauses her game and turns to look at me.

"What the heck are you covered in, Gray?"

"Well, it's a sugary mixture of chocolate, shame and fury. Some arsehole almost ran me over in the street."

"You're kidding me, right?" Harley rushes around the sofa and comes over to inspect me – for injuries, I imagine.

"Almost, Harl. I'm okay."

"So, what is this?" She fingers some of the cake off my jacket, sniffs it, then pops it in her mouth, moaning her appreciation.

"It *was* your birthday cake," I answer her with a sarcastic smile and one raised brow.

"What?! Who was it? Who trashed my cake?"

"Aww cheers, Harl. I almost got killed, but so long as you plot your revenge for the cake, it's all good." I pretend to be offended and wipe a fake tear from under my eye, feeling only slightly better that some prat almost ended me today.

She laughs at me, swipes another piece of mushed up cake from my jacket, then walks back over to the TV to continue shooting up adolescent teen boys, apparently satisfied that I'll live.

*

I spend the next couple of days completing my projects, texting Miles to join me as my plus one on Saturday night and shopping for another cake for Harley's birthday – though, nothing anywhere close to the awesomeness of her last one and it pissed me off even more.

It's Friday morning and I am tearing my hair out over this cake fiasco when someone knocks at my door.

Annoyed that I'm being dragged away from my laptop, I'm even more so when I open the door and find no-one standing there.

"What the fu--," I falter, staring at the floor near my feet.

Sat on my doorstep, is a pink and white box with a rope handle. My stomach flips and I'm a little too afraid to open the package.

I look up and down the landing, but no-one's there. I run to the window and see the tail end of a black car turning a corner, but that's nothing suspicious- it's a busy street. So, I spin back to the gift box. There's a note attached to it.

Edging over – I'm still wary of whatever is in this thing, and who left it here – I bend down and pick the piece of white card off.

Grace – a pretty name, for a pretty girl

I apologize once again

- C

Now who would this be off? Who the hell is 'C'?

The only person who would know anything about this packaging is Bella, and that douche...

Sexy, Businessman Adonis!

I tear the box open and there, nestled inside – and intact – is a cake in the shape of a PlayStation controller. But how the hell did he know?

Shit on a stick, he went into the bakery. *Yes, fabulous detective work, Grace. You could be a top P.I.,* but how fucking dare he throw his cash around in the hopes of making things all better? And so what if it might be working?

Read more by finding the book on Amazon

About the Author

Blair lives in the middle of England with her puppy dog (who's no longer a puppy), close to family and friends.

Her passion started, and continues, with reading – mostly Erotic Romances, but also Paranormal and other sub-genres.

When she doesn't have her nose in a book, she can be found shopping, be it online or around town, in a tattoo parlour, adding to her collection, or at home with her family or friends enjoying a movie, or gaming online.

Her hobbies include photography, gaming, painting, designing and making her own jewellery.

Unfortunately for Blair, she must finance her hobbies through full-time employment.

When she finds herself with a spare five minutes, she enjoys going out with her friends, taking small breaks around the country, and cooking.

Keep up to date with new releases and giveaways by visiting: http://www.facebook.com/BlairColemanAuthor

Other books by Blair Coleman

Allegra's Song

Graceful Damnation

Printed in Great Britain
by Amazon